Real Skin

By E.A. Green

Published By
Breaking Rules Publishing

Soft Cover – 10516
Published by Breaking Rules Publishing
Pompano Beach - Florida
www.breakingrulespublishing.com

Dedication

I wish to Dedicate this book to Jefferson Sage Jarrett, the Best friend a guy could Ever Have.

He decided one day that I had no choice but to create him a character in One of my books. I was going to make him a Father in K.O.A / KILLED ON ARRIVAL, but that character is the first one to die. His response, "as anyone would suspect," was No, I Don't Think So.

So, I decided to give him the Biggest Honor Of All. He will be REAL SKIN'S Main Character Detective Jarrett Jefferson. I sure hope that it all works out for him.

"Sadly," readers understand just how finicky we writers can be. Hang in there, Detective.

I would also like to Dedicate this book to All those who have a missing loved one. No One will ever understand the heartache that comes with never again being able to physically touch friends and members of your families who have vanished.

May Your Hearts be less heavy knowing that there are actual people who are not only praying for you but trying our hardest to keep our eyes aware of our surroundings, our ears opened for any calls for help and ours souls listening to that little voice which says PAY ATTENTION.

Today, "MORE THAN EVER," We must stop believing that someone right now will do that which I will pawn off on someone else tomorrow.

STEP UP AS IF IT WERE YOUR OWN MISSING AND PHYSICALLY LEND A HEART, HAND, AND EAR. THE LIVES OF THOSE THAT HAVE BEEN TAKEN ARE DEPENDING ON IT.

Sincerely E.A. Green / The Greenman.

At No Time was this Novel based on Actual Events.
Since this Novella is cast into the Future,
Any Resemblance to People's, Places or Persons
Was Purely Accidental,
Hopefully Not Coincidental,
And One Hundred Percent Unintentional.

The Table

Introduction

This thrilling detective story takes place in the Denver Metro. Arapahoe County Colorado to be exact.

Watch as Detective Jarrett Jefferson is given his most unusual case to date.

As he begins to track down the clues, a serial killer, "unlike any other," leads him to multiple missing persons, Eventually a member of his own family and an unimaginable crime that will lead to the unexpected involvement of a Major Company.

And that's only if the killer doesn't find him first.

Why Settle For

FAKE SKIN,

When You Can Have

REAL.

Look For A

REAL SKIN DEALER

Near You.

You can check out my other Global Selling Works at
https://www.breakingrulespublishing.com/bookstore.html

CH. 1
HAPPY BIRTHDAY DETECTIVE.

As Detective Jarrett was about to wrap up his shift, the last thing he needed today was another unexpected crime scene added to his already overloaded stack of work cases.

When the call for car Seventy-Six crackled over his radio, he was half expecting Becky from dispatch to be wishing him another Happy Birthday. With a large cake in her arms, that was the first thing the young gal greeted him with earlier that morning.

Being new to the force, Becky had no idea that this day was nothing to be celebrated.

The only plans JJ had today was getting off, grabbing the largest bottle of whiskey the liquor store had on his way home and drowning his sorrows while trying to forget that this day also marked the One Year Anniversary of his missing wife.

The last time she was seen, was while stopping off at their banks ATM before going shopping for his birthday gift last year.

And then nothing.

She literally vanished into thin air.

Her, their suburban, Becky's personal belongings such as her cell, purse, Two Grand and a few cloths, somehow walked off the earths face and was never seen again.

After three months, Arapahoe's Bureau of Investigation declared her a missing person and chalked the case up to a wife leaving her husband and not wanting to be found. Jarrett's known anger issues at the time had a lot to do with that verdict too.

Mr. Jefferson almost lost his job that day.

The Detective's violent outburst over the Bureaus refusal to continue searching for his wife sent him into a rage that ended up taking out the chief's entire office.

By the time they subdued JJ, every piece of furniture was damaged, windows were broken, and all the Supervisor's service awards laid smashed upon the tiled floor. If it hadn't been for Chief Rob Dutch standing up for him, Commissioner Wess would have fired Jarrett on the spot and had his beaten ass drug out the front doors.

Thanks' be to the Unknown Gods for luck, fate, and the fact that he was under extreme duress, his suspension only lasted for Three Months.

Just long enough to become a raving alcoholic.

It seemed that, "according to his few friends," a little bit of lunacy snuck into the picture at that time too. And that Crazy train costed him another Three months sitting at a desk before they would even consider allowing him back behind the wheel

That night's cleaning crew caught him in the act, "Red Handed," breaking into the chief's office after his fit earlier that day so he could get to his wife's cold case files. The half-gallon of rock gut whiskey in his hands didn't help the situation one bit; for his new desk job now came with a mandatory phycological evaluation, daily piss testing and at least ONE weekly trip to Alcoholics Anonymous.

It's only been Three Month's now since they finally suspended his desk duties and restored most of Mr. Jefferson's full duty privileges.

As the past replayed itself over in his head, JJ, "only known by his closest family and friends," unconsciously picked up the cars radio receiver and began to blindly respond to Becky's beck and call.

Detective Jarrett's presence was required at the Mile-High Storage units at Twenty-Four Thousand, Four Hundred and Fifty East Smokey Hill Road and East Wheatland's Parkway.

The Fire Department was called to put out a storage fire and ended up stumbling upon something they have no words to describe, and they are requesting Your Immediate Presence. She also wanted to know how long it would take before his arrival.

The dispatcher was needing to tell those who were still on scene something.

How long will it take?

HOW LONG WILL IT TAKE!

That seems to be the Million Dollar Question these days.

Everyone was wanting to know how long it will take before he Calms his ass down. How long will it take, before he lets go of Jean's case. How long will it take, before he stops drinking? How long will it take, before he declares her dead. "And The Best One Of All," was how long will it take, before he gets back up and starts dating.

And they wonder where he gets all of his stroke inducing rage.

Having to figure out how best to on the spot answer her invasive question was just enough to stoke those low burning embers.

He could take interstate Seventy, but that required crossing through Peoria, Byers, Strasburg while ducking and dodging a shit load of traffic. Even with lights running, he could be looking at a good hour to an Hour and a half.

Something JJ was not willing to chance because, "depending on the crime," there might be a possibility of wrapping up the scene in that time frame.

The quickest way would be at a top throttle speed without the chance of bumper to bumper traffic.

Since the Detective was out near Deer Trail, the fastest opportunity would be to head straight towards the Rocky Mountains. If he took Thirty-Eight Avenue and followed the sun that was about to sink, he could cut south on County Road One Eight One before continuing west on Knudtson Road.

Once Knudtson swings north onto Strasburg, all he has to do is get off at Quincy.

That only leaves about Twenty miles before he would arrive

at the scene.

If Jarrett had to guess, he could possibly make the Thirty-Six-mile drive in Thirty to Forty minutes.

And that's without lights and sirens.

But, what's the fun in that.

With lights and sirens, he figured that he could cut the drive down to Fifteen or twenty.

And like all cops with a Nascar complex, Detective Jarrett Jefferson told Becky to relay the message that it should only take him Ten to Fifteen minutes.

He was ready to get the Hell Out of Bum Fucked Egypt anyway.

Today has been one of those days wondering if the next suspects door that you knocked on, just happens to answer your inquisitiveness with a double-barreled shot gun after being up for the last seven days while all hopped up on meth.

You can always recognize one by that vacant, shrunken in skull look with all the missing teeth.

They literally are the walking, "No One's Home," undead.

It was also one of those days where you're bored out of your fucking mind because no one was home and even the family pet didn't give a shit to acknowledge your snooping presence.

Since the storage units are just a hop, skip and jump from the Aurora Reservoir, there's no telling what the fire brigade found. More than one corpse has been pulled out of that body of water.

There have even been cars, sunken boats and a Cessna Three Ten removed from the decent manufactured sized lake.

It was also one of the places a dive team had been sent to search for his missing wife. And that was due to the reservoir being square dab in their back yard. Detective Jarrett Jefferson's house address was Twenty-Six Thousand, Four Hundred and Forty-One East Harbor Drive.

The lake was, "literally," One Thousand feet from his back door.

A Perfect place to dumb a body, according to One of The Prick Detectives who had been assigned to handle Jean's missing case.

Officer Roland Rollins proclaimed that the Reservoir would have been his main choice, if he was needing to consider which options would have been the best when and if it ever came to getting rid of his own wife.

That confession always bothered Jarrett.

Especially when JJ put it into context after hearing Rollins and another Detective, "Vance Thomas," make a pack to off each other's wives while the Cadets were going through the academy together.

He's kept an open ear towards those two ever since.

Particularly after they were, "Magically," assigned as each other's partner.

The first thing a recruit learns in the honorable field of becoming an officer, is that cops always have your back. The second thing he learned was that dirty cops work together, and, "if under duel investigation," they Always Lie if needing too while ONLY watching their criminally involved individuality.

Like Rollins and Thomas would eventually be accused of.

Intent to commit a crime.

So, it's Highly Suggested that Cops should always be careful to keep their tongue In Check and Always Watch where they stepped. One never knows who's shit stained shoes are spreading and smearing the kind of crap that could end one's career Literally Overnight.

But Never those who sit upon the Top Rung.

"For some reason," the bodies waste always seems to continually roll downhill, while making sure to take out the dispensable who had been unknowingly singled out for takedown do to their Not Willing To Play The Department's Game of Unaccountability.

Mr. Jefferson caught a side swipe of that attitude after losing his mind over what Roland and Vance did to him and his wife Jean.

As Detective Jarrett sped down Quincy, the officer really wished that he could just head on home and have his first drink in over Three Months. That was the requirement if he was to stay on the streets and no longer doing desk duty.

If he was to get caught, the end result would be instant termination.

Sadly, how else is one supposed to handle not just the disappearance of their spouse, but her vanishing act also took place on his Thirtieth birthday.

That's why Mrs. Jefferson had Two Grand on her person.

She was getting him the perfect birthday present.

An LG, Seventy Two-Inch Smart TV with Blue Tooth Technology. It had every plug in imaginable and came with Memory Card and Flash Drive Capabilities. And Best Of All, he could now watch his shows And Movies IN THREE-D MODE.

Jean was supposed to have it completely installed by the time JJ came walking through their front door.

It was that excitement over the TV, "while filing her missing report," which caused a sense of suspicion to be raised in Detectives Rollins and Thomas.

Now when it came to their personal feelings towards Jarrett, everyone in the precinct knew that there was no love lost between the three. The dynamic duo has always felt that Jefferson was a little too high and mighty about his personal opinion of himself.

To the pair of Officers, Jarrett was always looking down his nose at them.

They were Absolutely Sure that NO ONE is That Squeaky Clean as JJ's attitude seemed to exude.

And Now, Arapahoe's Two Lead Investigators had been given an opportunity to prove it.

Their Gung-Ho Attitudes almost caused the pair to be thrown off of the case when it first began. That, and JJ's Incessive Proclamations Insisting Rollins and Thomas were refusing to keep the Brotherhood in Blues Motto of I've got your back.

The Two of them even went so far as to publicly threaten him, destroy paper evidence and tamper with the cameras at Jarrett and Jean's personal bank.

The last place Mrs. Jefferson was Positively seen.

She had stopped into Bank of the Rockies and had gone inside to make a withdrawal. The teller said JJ's Wife never did act as if she was in any kind of danger. In fact, the customer was bragging about the Awesome gift she was about to purchase for her husband.

The inside cameras facing the front doors were the first to show a heavy-set balding man being a gentleman, while holding the door open for her.

You can see him doing it again as they left together just a bit later.

After watching that video At Least A Thousand Times, "and interviewing Mr. Graves," it was pretty obvious that he had to run back outside to get his Identification.

He left it in his vehicle.

The banking individual said that he was in such a rush, "other than holding the door," he never paid much attention to the Detective's wife.

He didn't even notice what vehicle she left in.

That's if she left at all, Jarrett insisted.

Now when a department must decide between good cop and bad cop, that's where they close ranks and actually protect each other's backs. That is also where officers quickly find out just how many on the take cops there are.

Rollins and Thomas should have lost their jobs, been arrested, and spent a few years in jail themselves.

"But as usual," they were exonerated, and Jarrett ended up on a shrinks couch.

Pulling a gun on the Scum Bags before destroying the Chief's office later that night, did not do him any favors amongst those who Ran Arapahoe's Department of Investigation. If the safety had been off, at least One Of The Fuckers Would Most Certainly be dead right now.

The look on Rollins's face when the gun hammer clicked, still brings a warm sense of joy to JJ.

His Overly Shocked Expression had that melted wax look to it before the Dumb Ass realized that he was still breathing and unscathed.

That could not have been said about Officer Vance Thomas.

Detective Jarrett had no idea, "until at that exact moment," that some people have the bladder of a race horse.

It took a mop and bucket to soak up the gallon of piss that ran down his right leg.

They never talked again after that.

Both Detectives even went as far as to change work locations.

The last thing Jarrett heard was that they were denied entry into Douglas and most of the other surrounding Districts before the pair had No Other Choice but to settle on the only Law Enforcement Agency willing to take them.

Their misfortune turned out to be the running joke at JJ's precinct.

Rollins and Thomas slid out of here with their shit show and are now suffering from Montezuma's revenge.

The only county in south-east Colorado that was offering them a second chance.

The Sherriff's Department in Montezuma County.

As the Detective sped down Quincy Avenue, that creepy commercial from AWRS, "Androids with Real Skin," began to play on the radio. They were promoting a new angle for their androids and it was taking off like a Raging Forest Fire.

Seems everyone was liking the company's latest idea.

While Officer JJ was lost in the Icky factor, a Woman's Very Sensual Voice began to sell their latest gimmick.

Are you tired of making love to what feels like a kids Slip and Slide toy?

Here at AWRS, not all Synthetic Beings are the same.
Our Androids come with Goosebump Capabilities.
Why Settle For
FAKE SKIN,
When You Can Have
REAL.
Look For A

REAL SKIN DEALER

Near you.

The guys back at the precinct had been trying to sell JJ on that idea for the last six weeks.

His Best Friend John Randal had even offered to buy him a night with a love bot. "According to his lustful explanation," those bitches can be programed to do anything and everything. The rechargeable Coo-Coo clock was able to handle every position he threw at it.

John proudly proclaimed that he rode their machine to the point of almost breaking the dammed thing.

When he checked out of the sex parlor, the Android had to have a complete decontamination along with an entire memory wipe. The amount of porn and sexual positions downloaded for their encounter literally overloaded the bot's memory banks.

The look of disgust and response on the restoration gals face and lips was priceless.

You Nasty.

Just Nasty!

As the other guys tried their best not to let out a verbally amused smirk, Detective Randal followed that enjoyable proclamation up with a gut busting prediction.

If they thought my sexual encounter with that bot was bad, just wait until I screw one with Real Skin.

They are gonna have to decommission that bitch or let me take her home after we play.

I'm quite sure that No Amount of Scrubbing will remove the Floodwaters of juice I'm going to pump in, "and on," the walking Barbie Doll. That pornographic pronouncement was all the locker room talk it took to get a verbal FUCK-YES Response and a You're the Man John, from their fellow officers.

CH. 2
WHAT THE HELL.

Jarrett had been so caught up in the Remembrall antics from a few days ago, that he almost missed his turn onto South Harvest Road. His usual way home brings him north on East Four Seventy and East Aurora Parkway.

Either way, today's crime scene lays right along both of those well beaten pathways.

As the Mile-High Storage Units came into view, so did the dash clock that proudly displayed the fact that he had made record time.

That, "approximately," Forty Mile drive had been accomplished in under Ten Minutes.

Nine Minutes and Thirty-Six Seconds, to be exact.

Just as JJ pulled into the storage units' driveway, he quickly noticed that there was no coroner on site. There were however two Fire trucks, three vehicle units, "along with Six officers," and what could be the manager.

Oddly, there was No News Media.

What surprised Detective Jarrett Most, was the lack of hoses and gallons of liquid he usually has to wade through when it came to accessing a crime scene that ended up requiring the water boys.

This interaction had none of those qualities.

It did have something else though.

A look of Bewildering Puzzlement on the baker's dozen of first responders and law enforcement.

As Mr. Jefferson exited his vehicle, Officer James Porter

quickly approached the Detective so that he could give him the lay of the land.

He also wanted to shoot the shit a bit.

Even though the Officer and Detective have been absent from each other's routes, the last time they talked was when JJ's wife went missing. James was in charge of securing Jarrett's house as Rollins and Thomas proceeded to look for clues surrounding her unexplained absence.

Tweedledee and Tweedledumb also used that opportunity to trash every inch of the Jefferson's Two-story dwelling.

Officer Porter was getting Extremely Angry and Defensive for the Detective over how they were treating JJ. He was even willing to back Jarrett's ass after Jean's Husband almost went head to head with the Two On-Scene Detectives who were Willfully mishandling his case.

Porter, "Like JJ," could see the men for exactly what they were.

Nasty.

Volatile.

And Downright Dirty.

Both Leaches were what James referred to as ROTTEN TO THE CORE.

While the Investigators who were willing to cross the line went overboard, they also made sure, "One Hundred Percent," to let Jarrett know that they genuinely enjoyed ransacking his house.

With Unanimous Grins of Despicable Pleasure, both went so far as to show off the few pocketed pairs of Private Lingerie that their sticky fingers had STOLEN from Jeans undergarment drawer.

Officer Porter was Absolutely sure that there would have been an actual crime scene at that point if he hadn't of intervened between the Three when he did.

The last time James laid eyes on Detective Jarrett, he would have passed for a clean cut, "fresh out of the military," cadet. The guy walking towards him now was completely unrecognizable.

The Five-Foot Eight Detective looked as if he had lost somewhere between Thirty to Fifty pounds.

He was all beanpole now.

JJ's crew cut hair was also Well Past his shoulders by at least Two to Three inches this time around.

It also looked as if it has been weeks since it was last shampooed and conditioned.

The overgrown stubble on Mr. Jefferson's face was within a few days of becoming a good starting beard, while his clothes appeared as if they, "right along with him," had been sleeping on the floor for the past few weeks or Quite Possibly Months.

There was No Doubt that this last year had taken its toll on the widowed man.

"And to beat all," Today is the One Year Anniversary of Jean being declared missing.

It just so happened to be JJ'S BIRTHDAY TOO.

As Officer James reached out to shake Jarrett's hand, he could smell the answer as to why the Detective was working without a partner. He Reeked of Anger, Sadness and Distraught Bachelorhood.

No one in their right mind would want to work with someone who Just Might get Them Killed.

Something Porter knew All Too Well.

He also understood just how little it took to cause that kind of life destroying damage.

The Officer's personal life, "while, during and after his divorce," took years to recover from, as he and his Ex fought over every scrap of what was left of his then shambled existence.

Mrs. Porter even went so far as to seize all the food in their house.

Officer James never understood what was so special about making sure to take that one and only Fucking Bag of pinto beans.

She Hated Beans!

Once A Bitch, Always a Bitch, the last few of James's supporting friends would always tell him.

That advice usually came after: I Told You Not To Marry Her In The First Place, DUMB ASS.

It was while the two officers were getting reacquainted that Jarrett quizzingly asked why he was here. Since Arapahoe County's Coroner was nowhere to be found, Mr. Jefferson was just assuming that there were no bodies.

You would be correct, Porter responded.

Then why am I here, JJ wanted to know.

There is something inside the storage room that we have never seen nor come across before.

Something, You just have to see for yourself.

When the fire department responded, they were expecting a good-sized blaze. Instead, someone had installed an air conditioning window unit to keep what we found inside cold.

If the cooler's motor hadn't of burnt out, there's no telling just how long it would have been before someone found the hidden enigma within.

What they found next was something no one has ever come across.

We're still not too sure how to describe this Unusual discovery.

As the two men approached the unit's opened door, the first thing they noticed was the burnt smell of wires and the blackened soot that had encased everything within.

Along the Three walls Hung Two rows of Light boxes.

The kind a doctor uses when looking at X-rays of his patient.

There was also what appeared to be a spinning Antique barber's chair sitting perfectly in the rooms centered middle.

As other crime scene technicians began to look for DNA and Fingerprints that had not been damaged or destroyed by the smoke, a few of them were beginning to tackle the light boxes. The longest walls opposite from each other had Two rows of Six Light Boxes, while the back wall had Two rows of Five Light Boxes.

Now this is where the mystery of why dispatch had requested Jarrett's presence at the scene.

Each box held Thirty skin sample slides.

The kind that are used to look at shit under a microscope.

Those collecting the evidence were guessing that there were at least One Thousand and Two hundred skin samples.

Not only that, but they were all numerically labeled.

The first one he was able to observe after it was cleaned and checked for fingerprints was labeled Zero slash One slash Two slash Zero slash Eight slash Nine. The second one had the same labeling but with a different sequence.

One slash Zero slash One slash Nine slash Eight slash One.

This was definitely something a Detective doesn't see every day.

As Investigators began to spray for blood splatter and other things along the floors unblackened surface and corners, it quickly became apparent that someone had been busting a nut all over this place.

It was at that point, JJ new it was in his best interest to get out of the way and leave the rest to their hazmat team.

Taking this opportunity to do a bit of personal investigating on his own, JJ decided to walk up to the office so that he could see if the manager had any extra details about the unit, who rented it, when did he, she or they move in, and has he or anyone else helping to run the place ever met its occupier.

Jarrett was hoping for a Very Observant employee, but after entering the buzzer announcing door, the smoke-filled room of Marijuana, Tie Dye and Incense gave him all the answers that would be needed.

When I'm smoking The Good Shit, I Never Look Outside. MAN.

The room looked as if a Master of The Dyeing craft had been slaughtered and used for decoration before a Horticulturist Worst Nightmare was thrown into the Very Small and cramped quarters.

Among the Six Pot plants, there had to be at least another Hundred varieties of Fern, Wild Violets, Climbing Ivy, and many others that JJ had no idea what their names could be.

The Hippie Guru sitting amongst the indoor forest while

doing his daily meditation, secured the fact that This Stoner had no idea, "What-So-Ever," about the outside world and what took place on these premises.

Pot heads tend to mind their own business, so the chances of him seeing anything were extremely nil. And after mulling over his observations, the Detective quickly realized that this Marijuana smoker had no gold at the end of his chemically enhanced rainbow.

The, "I Know My Rights," hipster, also made sure to tell Jarrett that if he wants to look at the books or any surveillance recordings, Arapahoe's finest would be needing a court order first.

To which JJ replied, I will Certainly be back then.

Now here is where the Detective is different from most other investigators.

Back at the precinct, Jarrett Jefferson proudly displayed his Life's motto on a Very Large desk plaque which sat facing all those who needed to approach him.

Live By The Code.

His duty was to protect and serve, not hassle, and abuse those in their community.

Any other cop would have laid the law down to Mr. I Know My Rights.

If Rollins and Thomas were still around, Hippie Man would most certainly have ended up with a few bruises and a trinket or two would have Surely been broken inside his dwelling as they physically forced him to break the law.

But JJ wasn't like that.

And that pride in serving came straight from his dad.

Jefferson Senior was such an Honorable Man, that he was questionably demoted, "later getting fired," before he was willing to break that sworn code All Officers are required to take before they can receive their shield.

"On My Honor," I will Never Betray My Badge, My Integrity, My Character or The Public's Trust.

I Will Always have the Courage to hold Myself and Other Officers Accountable for Our Actions.

The Exact same Oath JJ swore and Now lives by himself.

As Jarrett climbed back into his unmarked Twenty, Twelve Dodge Ram Charger, he was still amazed that this car, "which was well over Ten Years past its prime," still had some kick and fight left in it.

It was also Detective Jefferson's very first; and sworn to be his last vehicle, ever.

He and Jean had made That Retirement Deal when her husband started his law enforcement career. When baby was put out to pasture or just happens to get totaled, "whichever came first," JJ was to follow suit also.

When the department received new cars a few years ago, "Unbeknownst to Jean," they attempted to do just that.

Chief Rob Dutch tried to send car Seventy-Six to the auction's chopping block, but after TWO FULL WEEKS of Jarrett squatting in it, Arguing Endlessly with Commissioner Wess and then out right putting a lean against it, they finally came to a deal.

So long as He got to keep the Charger, their Pain in The Ass Detective would buy the car, pay for All Repairs, "including tires," and cover half the cost of gas.

JJ, "for that added You Got A Deal," even went so far as to offer keeping it on his own full coverage insurance. But due to legal technicalities, the department, "just to cover their own asses," were required to cover that part if they so choose to let him have his way.

The price range difference in the Department's Favor, Instantly settled that debate.

Luck was finally on Jarrett Jefferson's side.

JJ Never Told Jean.

All she knew for those Two Weeks was that he was working undercover.

Now here it is, Eighteen Years Later; he and the car are still kicking up a storm.

In the past, the Precincts Detective could have just clocked out over the radio and gone on to his house that was less than Two minutes from where he's now parked.

But, today was JJ's last day of probation

And that's Only If his piss test comes out clean.

Rob Dutch, Arapahoe Counties Chief of Police was waiting back at the precinct for him.

They had an On Hands escort with a clear cup in his hands waiting to give JJ his Final hurdle before he would once again be considered a Full Duties Officer.

In the past, the Swat Team's Largest Bull of an Officer would personally see him into the bathroom, put on a rubber glove, and stand there holding the cup while JJ pulled out his cock and took an observed piss.

Jarrett was so ticked off after learning the rules of decorum that first time, that he Purposely whizzed all over the guys shoes.

The Gruntled Cyclone that Rumbled out of that bathroom, "which was soon followed up by Jefferson's black eye," said all that was needed, after the entire unit of Twenty heard the Violent slew of cuss words that flew from behind that closed restroom door.

Today, he was hoping for that same effect.

The Perfect Topping to Ice his cake.

But since it was his birthday, the department, "just in case," had already planned ahead. Dutch was going to make sure that he got the upper hand this time. And if Jarrett crossed the line, He could Finally kick his ass out the door for good.

Sadly, "on his behalf," the Chief had no idea that Detective Jarrett Jefferson had a sense of humor.

He also had No Idea that there was something closeted about his detective too.

As JJ walked through the front doors, Pete Kunkle met him with his rubber gloves and a nice clear specimen cup. After exchanging smiles and pleasantries, neither man had any idea that they were about to butter each other's biscuit.

The moment they walked into the restroom; the Detective quickly noticed that something new had been added to the mundane routine.

Officer Kunkle had not just one glove, but Two.

After putting on his gloves and explaining that since this was his last drug screen, JJ was to place Both his hands on his hips and the officer would be manually performing the rest of the maneuver for him.

Dutch needed to make sure that there would be no given opportunities for Jarrett to cheat.

Pete would be undressing him from the waist down, checking all cracks and crevices and then proceed to hold JJ's cock while he took a piss.

They both found a little bit of enjoyment in this maneuver; when the officer dually noted that Jarrett was starting to get a semi hard on, as his helper slowly began to stroke The Monsters current Seven inches.

While the cup began to fill, so did the Hardening soon to be Eleven Inch member in Pete's now ungloved hand.

The two seemed to be in perfect sink, as Officer Kunkle stepped from behind his charge, "and to the Detectives surprise," offered up something So Much Better than a pair of shoes.

Himself.

The clean-cut officer who was known for his manicured and spit shined look, also had another side to him.

Pete Kunkle was gay and considered himself a boy toy.

To Dominate Daddies, he was known as Here Piggy, Piggy.

Falling on his knees, the closeted cop, "Except to Chief Daddy Number One standing outside," began to bathe in the luke-warm liquid.

Pete Loved taking Golden showers.

He also Loved cleaning the spicket just as the tap was about to run out.

Before JJ could spit and shake out those last few drops, the little piggy at his feet sucked in his now hardened cock while making sure to drain that creamy jack pot load within. Afterwards, the Detective and Officer had a few laughs while cleaning up and sharing each other's reasoning for what just happened.

The Chief was trying to get rid of his ass.

But unbeknownst to the Departments head shot caller, JJ had just stumbled onto a case unlike any other. And by the time he is through solving this mystery, people will never look at their skin the same way ever again.

Kind of how the Chief appeared when both men came out of the restroom; Wet, Shirtless, Out Of Breath and Arm In Arm.

Completely Dumbfounded.

The radio advertisement currently playing over the stations public radio, said all that was needing to be said.

At AWRS,

"Even with your eyes closed,"

One can tell the difference between Our Synthetics and Those Other Latex Covered Ones.

Why Settle For
FAKE SKIN,
When You Can Have
REAL.
Look For A
REAL SKIN DEALER
Near You.

CH. 3
WE HAVE A CLUE.

As JJ and officer Pete Kunkle parted ways, the young man was barely around the corner when Chief Dutch lit into the guy. Detective Jarrett could hear Rob cussing Pete out because he was supposed to give them a reason to fire Jefferson, Not Pleasure Him.

The next thing that came from around the corner were the words; Your Sleeping On The Fucking Couch for the next Two Weeks, Bitch.

The Squads Haggard Detective almost busted out in an uncontrolled Bellowing Laugh after realizing the Pete was into Old and wrinkly man balls. JJ was wondering if he uses the Chiefs gray pubic hairs to floss with after he's done with his senior meal on wheels.

Since his shift should have ended over an hour ago, the widower decided a few more minutes on the clock wouldn't be a nuisance now.

Vickie should still be in the lab and he was curious to see if any other information has been gleaned from the weird evidence discovered at the storage unit. He also wanted to file the paperwork for the court order that would be needed just in case they found a crime.

It wasn't until he entered Vickie's lab, that he knew it would be better to just look around than bother her.

She did, "after all," have One Thousand and Twenty microscope slides to document and test for Blood, DNA and Genetic markers concerning whether the skin belongs to a male or female and which racial classification it most matches.

Seeing the frazzled look on her face said all that was needed.

Don't.

You.

Fucking.

Ask.

While JJ was doing his best to quietly snoop around without bothering the overly swamped woman; a small file that she had been reaching for, came flying his direction.

So Far, this is all the information I currently have for you Detective.

Take this and get out of my way before I decide to catalogue your ass under He asked Too many questions, so I killed The Bastard.

After gladly intercepting the small stack of papers hidden inside, Jefferson headed back upstairs to his office desk that sat in the middle of the Department's Main room. He would quickly fill out the hoping to be delivered court order and then see what treasures were hidden inside the manila folder.

And that is exactly what the information inside looked like.

Map codes to a treasure.

Those numbers ran in a most unusual sequence.

Zero slash Two slash Zero slash Nine slash Eight slash One.

The next one was listed as One slash One slash Two slash Seven slash Eight slash Two.

That random numbering went on for Eleven Pages.

As he sat at his desk, Detective Jarrett just happened to notice that Chief Rob Dutch must have made up with his boy toy. He was walking out of the precinct with his arm draped over the young Detective's shoulder.

JJ also, "Thanks to Pete Kunkle," had some ammunition to use against his superior just in case it ever came down to a faceoff between the Two Law Enforcement Officers.

While sitting at his desk and running down the rabbit hole of what ifs, his subconscious picked up the whispers between His Best Friend John Randal and another Detective by the name of Tom Long.

Tom was amused by JJ's eternal stare and was commenting to John, there he goes again.

Just like Alice Through The Looking Glass, the guys were running a secretive betting pot that was dished out to the winner on a weekly basis.

With at least One witness present, they would time just how long it took before Jefferson caught his rabbit and returned from the
looking glass's other side.

This week, JJ actually set a record.

Twelve Minutes and Forty-Five seconds.

So Far, Miss Vawn down in the lab held that winning spot.

While JJ stared blankly into the secretive code of One Thousand and Twenty numbered slides, his mind was sitting in the old barber chair back at the storage unit and trying to imagine what would take place there when the owner came to visit.

As the image of him sitting in the leather barber style chair began to visualize itself, there was No Doubt about this being a sexual fetish.

An Illegal one; on the other hand, was still up for grabs.

Whoever this individual is; they must be working at some kind of medical lab, a diagnosis facility or they were stealing these unusual medical specimens for their own sexual pleasure.

Either way, this kink was unheard of in his repertoire of things to get off on.

Other than the evidence they already have, the burnt-out motor in the window unit that had caused all the commotion was the next thing to be tracked.

Something else that would be requiring a court order.

The department just needed an actual crime scene. Only that would allow him to investigate this any further.

It was while climbing back out of his rabbit hole that JJ finally took notice over just how late it actually was. The sun had set hours ago, and the Liquor stores closed their doors about Thirty Minutes prior.

That turned out to be an unintentional blessing anyway.

Jarrett was willing to bet that there would be a surprise piss test waiting for him first thing tomorrow morning.

Especially, with his birthday being the exact same day Jean went missing.

Today.

More than likely, the Chief was banking on him fucking this moment up. JJ was so looking forward to seeing his disappointed face Tuesday morning when he realizes that Detective Jarrett Jefferson wasn't going to play his game of cat and mouse.

"So," that gut rotting whiskey he loves so much, will just have to wait on another day, time, and place.

By now, he was pretty sure the Chief also had other things on his mind right now too.

His Little Piggy, Piggy.

Just imagining Pete referring to Dutch as Daddy, was enough to make JJ forcefully swallow the mouthful of regurgitation that tried to make its way out and into the waste basket by his desk.

As the unkept Detective decided that it was time to start heading for the door, John Randal, "while wildly waving his arms on that Six Foot Two frame of his," Loudly demanded that His Best Friend needed to come over and see him before walking out that front exit and going home.

When Mr. Jefferson first arrived that morning, Becky and a few others tried to corner him. But, his excuse of having to drive out to the far corner of Arapahoe County gave him a quick way out.

But not this time.

His Thirty First Birthday started the official countdown before he turned Forty. The running joke was that he better keep an eye out because this is when the bodies check engine light starts to blink off and on.

As the small group of ten began to sing their version of a middle school's happy birthday song, all JJ could hear was his own damnation for letting Jean get his Surprise birthday gift All

Alone.

What Happened To Her Was His Fault.

And since it involved having a Television Set, not one of those Monstrosities has ever stepped foot in his house since.

While the Happy Birthday to you, You look like an Ape and You Smell like one Too was winding down, the Detective new exactly what they were referring too. The smell of Piss and Pete had not only permeated the hair in his nostrils, but Jarrett's clothes also carried that reek of masculinity into every corner of their precinct.

And just when the Birthday Boy thought it couldn't get any worse, the gift Randel handed to him proved otherwise. The guys had All chipped in and bought him a Golden Pass to one of AWRS's try it before you buy it Theme Saunas.

This not only gave JJ Full Access to any of the Bot's, but he had his pick of themed rooms too.

And if he so chose to get a Platinum upgrade, the only thing that could touch him then would be Real Skin and not some latex inflatable Coo-Coo Clock.

To this day, JJ's still not sure why John Randal calls them that.

After a couple of arm and stomach jabs, a few cuss words of encouragement and the THREAT of You Better Not Toss or Waist This, Randal wrapped his best friend in an air choking bear hug.

John then Proclaimed his Love for the man and just how much he cared for JJ.

He also expressed how Extremely proud he was of Jarrett for fighting his demons and living to tell about his battles and recovery.

A lesson every man and woman in their department needed to learn.

It was then John whispered his last surprise between the Two friends, I've already upgraded your gift to the Platinum card.

You Can Thank Me Later.

But there would be no thanking Randal after JJ sees that

John had one last surprise for him if he so chose to go.

The synthetic had already been ordered ahead of time and was supposed to resemble Jean's picture that John had sent in advance.

As Jarrett said his goodbyes before heading home, the thought of being alone on this night was causing Overwhelming feelings of loneliness, despair, and a desire to just crawl into a corner before slitting his wrists.

But, a second walk down that road was Out Of The Question.

If you wish to stay alive and be a part of law enforcement, one needs to learn that they are not on their own. And when that lesson just happens to take place to either a man, "or woman," a person must learn how to stand and fight for what they believe in.

JJ just had to snicker at that one, because that kind of thinking is exactly what put him in the situation he's had to spend the last year crawling out of.

He Believed that Jean would Never have left him and something Really Bad happened to her.

One way or the other, he would prove it to everyone.

Even if that revelation required his last and dying breath, Mr. Jefferson WAS Going To Show Them All that they had been Horribly Wrong.

As Becky packed him a piece of his birthday cake to take home, the shy girl whispery asked the Detective if he was maybe in the mood for some private company later. She might not be some fancy sex bot, but the dispatcher guaranteed JJ that she had the stamina of one.

And that's when she saw Jarrett do something unlike the man she has come to know.

He actually blushed.

Jefferson reminded her of Professor Waddell, the man she had a crush on and who More Than Willingly took the woman's virginity her freshman year at college. The weird response Becky received from the Detective who could have passed as a pot smoking college professor himself, came as quite a shock.

I do not think my wife will approve Miss. Grove.

She understood that the man was still in morning but being the new kid on their block, Becky had no idea that Jean went missing on his birthday. That learned Too Late secret was the reasoning to why a few of the guys had unsuccessfully tried to hush her smart-ass response to his unacceptable answer.

I Sure Hope the Coo-Coo clock can pleasure you better than I could have, because I would Most Certainly have fucked your dick off.

Your Loss Mr. Jefferson.

That hurt little ball of pride then made sure to verbally huff her displeasure as they both went their separate ways that evening.

Becky did seem to get a spark in her step though, after Randal popped off; if your itch is still needing to be scratched when I clock out here in a bit, I'll take care of you little lady. Jarrett found out later, that the pair never made it past the department's storage closet before mops and brooms began to fly against the interiors four walls.

Tom Long laughed for weeks over the fact that their encounter reminded him of that scene in Porky's where the Two gym teachers screwed each other on a stack of jock straps.

John revealed that, "just to squelch her moaning cries," he tried shoving his own crotch stained jock into her mouth.

A move that had No effect on the woman's Wall Vibrating WAILS.

Since that movie was at least twice Becky's age, she never understood the secretive joke after the guys in JJ's department went behind her back and nicknamed the woman Lassie. The howling laughter that would randomly erupt from their gatherings always went right over her Five Foot Two head.

Becky would most certainly have gone on a killer warpath if she were to ever learn that, "after their Lustful encounters," Detective Randal always made sure to share every last juicy detail that occurred between the pair.

Miss. Grove's," unbeknownst to her," had become the

departments secretively lusted after porn queen. The Dispatcher also had no idea that John Randal had tapes that could prove every last pornographic word he shared In Full Detail, with any and all if his guy friends concerning their sinful romps.

The Scene that was most requested by his buddies, was when John hog tied her and spent that entire weekend expanding the depths and limits of Miss. Grove's hungry vagina with his Boxing Glove Sized Hands.

While JJ grabbed the rest of his things and started to head out, the Detective realized that, "other than the cake," he hasn't eaten all day.

According to the pocket of receipts he has been carrying around for the last week, it's been at least two days since an actual meal has crossed his lips. Jean Always said that Twinkies, chips, and soda, IN NO WAY count as a Real Meal.

She was even willing to withhold sex from their relationship after finding out that he's been lying to her while starving himself on nothing but sugar.

Until her husband sat down and ate a physical dinner requiring at least Two vegetables, the only action he was getting would be from Rosy Palms and her Five Daughters.

That was one of the main reasons he Loved Jean so much.

The woman Never took his I Do Not Want To, "Or No," for an answer.

As JJ pulled the only Female now left in his life onto the East Bronco's Parkway, he and the Dodge Charger settled down into their lets head home routine.

After having to live in her for Almost Two Weeks, he and Adeline knew every last intimate inch of each other. His needing a chiropractor for his back, screamed at the Detective for over a month after forcing his vertebrae to bend and sleep in such unimaginable positions.

Not even the Kama Sutra chanced some of those spine breaking moves.

The last thing JJ conscientiously heard before getting onto

C-Four Seventy, was another sex add from Androids With Real Skin.

At AWRS, we strive for

THE REAL EXPERIANCE.

If your lover squeaks like an over inflated balloon,

It's time to grow up.

The only noise one should be hearing while having sex,

Is Skin rubbing against Skin.

Why Settle For

FAKE SKIN,

When You Can Have

REAL.

Look For A

REAL SKIN DEALER

Near You.

And with that last unsolicited advertisement, JJ turned off the radio, opened the glove box and tossed his upgraded platinum ticket to AWRS's playgrounds into its darkened depths of junk, bills, and fast food wrappers.

The only thing he wanted touching his skin tonight, was the last set of lingerie that Jean planned to wear for his birthday the day she went missing.

CH. 4
INTO THE DARKNESS.

As usual, the drive back to his Two-Story pad sped by quicker than a virginal male pops his first load while blowing his cherry in the bathroom. Except this night, there wasn't any excitement arriving home to an empty house with no one to play or celebrate with.

The first thing JJ did; no sooner than he drove up the driveway to an already opening garage door, was to break out in tears.

There staring back at him was Jean's Suburban.

The vehicle had been found that next morning still sitting in the banks parking lot.

There was a good chance Jarrett would have found it that night he realized she was missing, but he was ordered to stay at home so that he would not contaminate the scene or appear as a suspect.

The Chief However did not want his Detective to accidently taint any evidence that might be found as Arapahoe's department of investigation began their county grid search for her.

That turned out to be one of JJ's Longest Nights.

Kind of how tonight was already starting to feel.

Leaving the Dodge Charger sitting outside, Mr. Jefferson decided to do something that he hasn't done for the last Three Months now. He opened the stored vehicle's driver side door and climbed in.

When Jean went missing, this was where he prayed and held

his daily talks with her.

Sadly, that relationship between him and her suburban did not start until the vehicle was searched, printed and evidence collected.

THREE MONTH'S AFTER SHE DISSAPEARED!

As JJ's tears turned into a torrential downpour, so did his anger.

He beat the top portion of that steering wheel So Hard, it physically started to crack and bend. While the wheel began giving to its reformation, his anger, hatred, and frustrations came pouring out like those of an Enraged Silver-Back Gorilla.

The largest part of that grieving resentment came in the form of WHY.

Why couldn't she have waited until he got home.

Why were the heads of his department refusing to take him serious.

Why can't they see that she Never would have left him.

And the biggest one of all, "which finally forced the vehicles steering wheel into a Ninety-Degree Bend," was WHY CAN'T I FIND YOU JEAN.

While the Detective's bloodied and bruised hands locked their viselike death grip onto the wheel, a years' worth of drowning anguish exploded from the depths of her husband's lost and mourning soul.

It was that overwhelming reverberation which finally caused JJ to take account of his surroundings.

He was half expecting one of his neighbors to call the cops over his insane reaction after coming home, but thankfully he had subconsciously shut the garage door before losing his overwhelmed mind.

Having the house all to himself this night was not helping matters either.

Everywhere he looked, there was evidence of her presence.

Pictures of either herself or of them; were placed on shelves, coffee, and side tables, while hanging upon the walls in almost every room too. Even her Hand stitched Initialed bedtime slippers still sat by the back door; where JEAN would exchange them for her, I'm Going To Run Errands Now, sneakers.

That's another reason why JJ was ABSOLUTELY CERTAIN His Wife DID NOT LEAVE HIM.

Those warm, fur lined moccasins were like gold to her.

She would leave the financial retirement money in their hidden safe, "which she did," before ever leaving behind those cozy foot warmers.

As Jean's husband continued into the kitchen, the evidence of a man who desperately needed his wife was everywhere. There were dishes sitting in the sink that had enough encrusted food left over on them, that they could have been declared a part of an archaeological dig.

It was obvious that the tiled floor hadn't been swept or mopped since the day of her disappearance.

And even with the refrigerator door closed, something besides the trash pile was adding that extra stench of retching disgust to the rooms overpowering aroma. That's why the sliding glass doors were always the first thing opened once JJ returned home.

There also seemed to be an article of clothing placed every other step upon the stained, unvacuumed and carpeted floor.

The dwellings first floor was pretty much a pigsty of utter disgust.

While the bachelor stood over the overflowing sink, "waiting for his frozen meal to cook in the disgustingly uncleaned microwave," he vacantly stared at the unwashed silverware before picking out a fork and running it under the cold water.

Jarrett would have liked to have used some hot water, but he forgot to pay the gas bill that was late once again.

Until he could take care of that tomorrow, a cold shower it would be then.

Oh Well, Happy Birthday to me was JJ's mumbled response to his stupidity of not paying attention to the important things in life that are a Must Be Done, if one so wishes to live in peace and comfort.

But there would be no peace.

Especially, This Night.

Taking out his frustrations in a physical outburst once more, the Chicken Pot Pie stood no chance as it was flung across the kitchen counter and out into the opened aired living room.

That's when the Cries of WHY, JEAN, WHY: Erupted from her husband's tortured spirit Once Again.

WHY.

WHY!

WHYYYYYYYYYY!!!!!!!!!!!!

As JJ decided to just go ahead and take himself up the glass encrusted stairs; the long-sleeved button shirt that he had been wearing for the last two days was slowly removed and ended up joining the other food covering disasters that lain upon the bacterial plagued carpet.

It was while the broken husband trudged his way up the stairs of glass slivered land mines, that Mr. Jefferson finally took notice of all the damage that he had caused to its supporting wall.

There were places where picture frames once hung but only their shadowed outlines remained. Other areas of the flattened structure contained fist prints or punched out portions of what used to be eggshell painted dry wall.

The Few pictures that were still in hanging existence, were either hung at odd angles while remaining, "somehow," whole or their glass and frames had been annihilated by burst of anger and unfettered frustration.

JJ was a walking Disaster Movie in the Making.

This is why His Best Friend John Randal was trying to convince him that he still needed help and to continue seeing the Department's shrink. And if he wasn't comfortable seeing the Counties I will Decide if Your Crazy or not doctor, he should still see one on his own dime and time.

At least that way, what was said would remain private and not end up being a part of his performance record back at their Precinct.

Detective Randal was fearful that he was going to lose his

friend and was dreading the day someone came up to him with the news that JJ had went ahead and blew his Fucking brains out.

And if that scenario didn't pan out, John was Absolutely certain that he would just end up watching Jarrett drink himself into an early grave.

He was Hoping to be a part of Neither outcome.

That battle of wills, "Six Months Ago," was the main reason JJ's Best Friend never stepped foot into the house again.

He Was Forbidden.

Once Jean's husband tripped and stumbled his way down the hallway of random obstacles that had been thrown wherever, the scraggly Detective decided to just go on ahead and take himself an Ice-Cold shower.

JJ was hoping that the hypothermia inducing water might somehow dull his overly strained emotions.

Before turning on the shower, he thought It best to go ahead and remove the laundry basket of unwashed clothes from the tub. The tossed and empty bottles of soap, shampoo and toilet rolls soon followed suit.

Right out the master bathrooms double doors and onto the bedroom floor.

He actually got lucky this time, because it all landed were he threw it instead of knocking over a Knick-Knack or an overly piled clump of whatever and blocking his one-persons path that zig-zagged its way across the rooms entrance door right into its restroom of Horrors.

The Lavatories unwashed and pissed stained floor held Mr. Jefferson firmly in place, as he dug his way through the bags of trash that were placed in and on the bathrooms sink counter.

If his missing wife ever saw this, Jean would have been appalled.

There's a good chance that she would have shoved her husband's head up his Dumb Ass over such inexcusable behavior too.

WHAT ARE YOU THINKING, Would have been her Screamed questioning.

A years' worth of beard and stubble layered every inch of that trash covered counter, while tons more stuck to the bottoms of JJ's bare feet as he was getting ready to shower.

And as for the toilet, it has held days of unflushed piss and shit before he remembered to hit its Be Gone Handle. The brown stains of fecal matter and encrusted minerals that used to flow from Jarrett's liquor drowned liver, encased the inner bowl.

The time it would take to clean that Hazmat Disaster would be better spent just buying a new one and replacing it at the hands of a plumber. And that's if the Tradesman is willing to get anywhere near that contaminated catastrophe.

As the Detective finished stripping down into his birthday suit and stepped into the body numbing water, the voice screaming in his mind was having none of it.

Besides that Main question of WHY, JJ's other heavily laden query was WHERE.

Where Are You Jean.

Where.

WHERE.

WHERE!

Supposedly, Arapahoe's Department of Investigation had exhausted all leads.

The cameras outside their bank were broke and not working that day. Their replacements had been scheduled for that following morning.

The ATM, "for the moment," was temporarily placed inside the establishment's entrance.

Front Range Banking had done this for the safety of their customers.

Jean walked in, did her business, then walked out.

She was Never seen again.

When the suburban was searched, they found a dry cleaner's stub for a weeks' worth of just her clothes. Jean's purse, the garments, cellphone, her refilled medications, and the Two Thousand Dollars JJ's Wife just withdrew, Were All Missing.

Detective's Rollins and Thomas kept Jibber Jabbing JJ;

saying that she had a Sancho on the side, and They were willing to bet that she left with him.

Unbeknown to the two shitheads, Jarrett considered that stupidity their first strike.

If the Detectives continued Proclaiming and Creating False Rumors, all bets would be off as to whether someone was going down with a broken nose, bloodied lip Or Worse.

While JJ stood there taking a piss in the cold running water, he watched the cleansing liquid swirl its way down the blackened tub stained drain. There was a good chance that this uncleaned environment was the reason as to why he was currently fighting Athlete's foot.

God he missed his wife.

They may have had a many of quarrels over his sloppiness, but Dam could that woman keep a clean house.

JJ's uncleanliness when it came to his domain was the Main reason why it took over Three Years of courting before she finally said yes. That, and the fact that his future wife threatened to get that show Hoarders involved if he was to ever pull such bullshit on her and HER House.

As Jean's heartbroken husband dripped his way over to their bed; the sheets that haven't been changed since she last slept in them, received his wet and tired body as he sat down on the sleep comforters edge.

He was just about to lay down and curl up in the grime scented sheets when Mr. Jefferson remembered the one thing that would not be forgotten on this night.

Crawling over the unmade bed and making his way to the Master Closet, there hanging on a silk covered clothes hanger was the powder blue baby doll lingerie dress that she had JJ pick out for his birthday.

Jean was supposed to wear it that night after going out on the town in celebration of Mr. Jefferson making it unscathed for another full year as an Officer of the law.

Yeah, Well That Never Happened.

Her Husband's been So Upset and Dealing with the disaster his life has become after her disappearance, that tonight would be the first time it has ever been touched by Jarrett's hands.

Gently carrying the thigh length garment over to the bed, "hanger and all," JJ tenderly placed the see-through material in the spot where Jean would have laid. Throwing his right arm across her pillow and setting the hangers loop in the pivot of his arm, the saddened widower turned to look at the vacant spot where his wife should have been.

And then he began to speak.

I Miss You Jean.

I Miss and Love You So Much.

My Heart Breaks thinking that I never really told you Just How Incredibly Important You Were To Me.

If I Never conveyed that You were My One and Only, I am So Sorry.

You were the light to my darkness; and every day that your shining face greeted me with that dimple crested smile, I knew that everything would be all right.

I Miss You and that smile.

If I was in a rut or swimming blinded in the work that I promised to never bring home, your stern laugh of You Said remembrance always steered me back to where I belonged.

Your storm calming port was always there to receive my battered and worn spirit.

Where Are You Jean?

Where Did You Go?

What happened to you after walking out our bank.

As question after question started to batter down the hatches, JJ's raw emotions began to beat at his fractured and unhealable heart once again.

Every part of his physical being was doing everything it could to convince the Detective that his wife was somewhere out there and in Desperate need of her husband's intervention. No one, "Not even the department nor his Best Friend," would ever be able to convince him otherwise.

Until either Jean or her body is found, Mrs. Jefferson would Never have walked away from her husband.

He Was ABSOLUTELY Positive of it.

Just as much as the tears Rolling down Jarrett's face were overwhelmingly saying how incredibly sure they were over his unconditional love for Jean.

Mr. Jefferson had no qualms over the fact that Mrs. Jefferson was his Soul Mate.

And he was hers.

That empty and ripped out portion of Her husband's spirit would Never be healed until he found her.

Taking that last deep sigh of the night before falling asleep, Jarrett Jefferson wrapped his left arm around the baby blue dress and pulled it in tight. It was his birthday after all; and whether she was here or not, JJ was going to cuddle with his missing wife.

The last words spoken after he turned off the lights were, I Miss You Honey bear.

I Truly Do Miss & love You.

CH. 5
WE HAVE ANOTHER CLUE.

With that next morning's sun rising over the eastern plains of Colorado, the Detective was extremely anxious to get back to the department.

This unusual case was not something one would expect to run across.

It was Definitely Not your run of the mill scenario.

After stopping to grab what every cop is accused of, JJ arrived at the office with a Large Container of cream and sugared coffee, just like the very first cup his grandmother introduced him too.

Two glazed doughnuts and a crumpled receipt inside a partially read newspaper that had been brought from the front stoop of JJ's house, accompanied the still unkept and dirty clothes smelling officer also.

Tossing the newspaper down before placing his coffee and sugar filled delights onto his work station, the hidden receipt from the Morning Joe Shop partially slid from its hiding place.

Other than the items he personally placed on the desk; Detective Jarrett noticed that a sticky note had been attached to the file Vickie had given him the night before. The envelope that held One Thousand and Twenty numbers which had been associated with the skin slides.

All it said was call me, ASAP.

Vickie Vawn.

And after a few bites of glazed wonderful and a couple of sips from his sugar laden drink, JJ picked up the phone and dialed down to the lab that was contained in the building's basement.

He was just about to hang up after all the excessive ringing, when she finally picked up.

Taking this moment to be a gentleman, Jarrett made sure to say good morning and introduce himself just in case she didn't recognize his voice.

It's also best to be polite to the one who has your case by the balls.

After a quick back and forth banter, JJ went ahead and asked Vickie about the sticky note on his desk. He was wondering if there had been enough time to find some evidentiary results.

To which she quickly replied, yes.

Yes I Do.

As of right now, I do not see a crime.

The few DNA results that have come back, show that some of the slides belong to individuals who had donated their bodies to science.

So that explains why there are skin samples pertaining to them.

And then we found others that belong to those that had been declared legally dead at either a mortuary or hospital.

Samples of their skin would have been taken too.

The only crime that I am willing to admit too, may have been committed by some unauthorized person who had taken these for their own pleasure. Something that is DEFFINATELY Against a Company's policy when it pertains to material that is considered a Bio-Hazzard.

Other than that, and the fact I was told what was being done with them, I would be willing to say that a murder investigation isn't required at this time.

When we get the rest of your samples back, "and if things change," I will let you know.

Not wanting to deal with his Chief just yet over these early and unpromising results, JJ looked over the paperwork that would be needed for a court order just in case things turned, and he was still curious and needing to figure out what all the number sequencing meant.

While slipping down the rabbit hole that was drawing him into trying to figure out the number puzzle; somewhere in the back of his subconscious JJ heard Randal shout, Time Starts Now.

AWRS was also pronouncing their Latest and Greatest Advancement over the public radio station that the department was tuned into.

At Androids With Real Skin, We are upping the game.
Not Only do our Synthetics Look Real,
They Feel REAL.
You can now get them with Tribal Details Also.
We also carry a Tattoo and Pierced line.
Toss that Imitation Skinned Doll away and go for an upgrade.
Why Settle For
FAKE SKIN,
When You Can Have
REAL.
Look For A
REAL SKIN DEALER
Near You.

Now, the thing about rabbit holes are their randomly revealing paths.

As Detective Jarrett Jefferson sat staring at the page of numbers and slashes, the receipt that had slipped out from inside his newspaper just so happened to catch his eye.

The cashier that had taken his coffee order had signed his initials, "JJ," on the receipt before handing it over to the barista. His initials had accidently added a few extra slashes between the date stamped on the paper.

Instead of Zero Seven slash Zero Two Slash Twenty Thirty, it looked like Zero slash Seven slash Zero slash Two slash Two slash Zero slash Three slash Zero.

The numbers in the storage unit that were related to the skin slides were not random or some form of code, they were physical dates. JJ now had One Thousand and Twenty Actual days, months and years that could make finding those attached to the samples easy.

He was never expecting to eat any more of his birthday cake that was still in the break room, but he would be more than pleased to have and share a piece in celebration with this Awesome turn of events.

There might not be a crime just yet, but this win made him feel that he had somehow upped the game.

This was also such Great news that he was not willing to just ring up Vickie.

This kind of news needed to be shared in person.

It would also show the lab technician just how much he considered her a team player and not just some broad with a degree on the wall and a chip on her shoulder.

That was just how Detective Randal and his side kick Tom Long looked at women.

With Total Disdain in their hearts and lust dripping from their I'm going to Fuck You whether you like it or not Loins.

Not something Jarrett ever wanted to be a part of.

The look JJ first received from Vickie after walking into her latest autopsy that was being recorded, was not what he was expecting. She was quite upset that he showed no common courtesy or professional respect as he excitedly barged into the room.

Miss. Vawn quickly calmed down though, after realizing that Jarrett had new clues and she was actually in need of a piss break herself.

As she quickly excused herself and told him to wait right here, a new delivery of mail and results walked through the door. The Officer was hoping that if anything in the manila enveloped just happened to pertain to his case, let it be something declaring the storage unit an actual crime scene.

While standing in the autopsy room, Mr. Jefferson had forgotten just how overwhelming the smell amongst the dead can be.

The body lying on the dissection table appeared to be a

young woman seeming to be between the Twenty-Five to Thirty-Five age range.

She also looked as if she was healthier than a horse.

It was quite obvious that the Five Foot Two Brunette worked out and appeared to have taken extreme care of her body. From the opened rib cage, all organs were in their rightful places and there didn't seem to be any signs of trauma or disease.

If JJ has learned anything in his Many Years at the department; no matter how well or extreme someone tries to take care of themselves, when it is your time, it's your time.

Too bad he thought to himself, those perky tits must have cost a fortune.

And once Vickie is done dissecting the body, the silicone gel packs in those Double-D bombshells were going straight into the trash.

Where's your sugar daddy now, Jarrett wondered.

Using her dead body as the main interest as to why he was snooping and moving around the room, the Detective was just within an arm's length of the newly arrived folder when Miss. Vawn burst back into the morgue's room of dismemberment.

The look on her overworked face said that she was ready for some good news.

And after JJ pointed out that some more evidence had arrived while she was out of the room, the two servants of the Arapahoe Counties Investigation Departments decided to take a seat and see what the cat dragged in.

Before the newly arrived package was opened, the lab technician was interested in hearing what JJ found first.

After giving a long, but what should have been the condensed version of his story; the Detective explained that the odd numbers and slashes turned out to be the day, month and year associated with the skin sample slides.

To Vickie, that made Perfect Sense.

Every last piece of evidence in this room was always stamped with the date, time, and the initials of who performed whatever task was required from the sample at that moment.

The odd thing about what they found was she has never seen a document stamped like the ones they discovered. The extra slashes between the numbers seemed like a confusing overkill that would not have been accepted or tolerated in her profession.

Space was important and all the extra slashes took up the already small area that may be needed for when a longer explanation was needed.

This also means that someone without medical filing experience was either stealing evidence before it reached were it was supposed to go, or they were taking from the Bio-Hazzard waste baskets where bad samples are disposed of.

If this case were pursued, neither would be a good outcome for those companies who just might end up being connected to the slides.

No matter how small, stealing any kind of bodily tissue was considered a felony.

As the two sat pondering the outcome on what they are currently working with, Miss. Vawn couldn't help but notice that Jarrett wasn't able to keep his eyes off today's mail.

She could have reached over at that point and took a moment to see what was in the envelope, but Vickie was also having fun teasing the Detective. The Technician would presume to be grabbing for it, before acting like something else was sidetracking her during their discussion.

When she finally noticed that JJ was approaching his breaking point, the public servant grabbed the days mail and proceeded to satisfy Mr. Jefferson's hunger for the information that was hidden inside.

At first, Vickie's facial expressions only revealed that there was nothing unusual about the findings.

But, that response quickly changed once she began to read the second page of results.

JJ: we actually have something here, She Excitedly Responded.

So far, "out of the One Thousand and Twenty slides," we are now looking at Thirty Missing Persons that have been declared dead, and another Twenty that are declared missing. There is NO WAY IN HELL, a lab would have such skin samples unless that was the last place they were seen before vanishing.

So as of right now, we have samples from a group that donated their bodies to science.

A grouping of individuals that have been legally declared dead.

And a group that has been identified as missing.

We also have results that there are no DNA matches in the system for another set of the slides.

This mystery grouping could only fit into One Category. The Unknown.

As the two coworkers sitting next to each other began to ponder the possibilities of where this case was heading, JJ Happily understood that he now had enough evidence to file a warrant.

Arapahoe County could finally search the records and video surveillance for any evidence Mile High Storage may have pertaining to what has become a White-Hot Investigation.

Also, Jefferson could now start matching dates to the declared and undeclared missing.

Since it now appeared as if their suspect was not working in a lab, how and what was he doing to those who's skin samples were decorating the storage units three walls. And how was this person getting the slides of those that never should have been in his possession.

Donated bodies to science usually end up at colleges so that future doctors can have something to practice on before they ever get the opportunity to slice and dice on the real thing.

The cast net to this mystery was going to end up being a Very Large Dragnet.

That list would now cover morgues, coroner services, funeral homes, colleges, and any other places that would have access to the dead.

Before the Detective could head down any of those paths, there was one trail he had to travel first. The warrant in his hand needed to be signed off by his Chief and then it also had to be approved by a local judge.

Chief Rob Dutch started to come off as his usual Hard Ass until the missing person's evidence revealed the truth that there was No Way any of those slides could have come from a lab.

Any Labs involvement in such matters were pretty much off the table at this point.

And unless a morgue or college was involved, the Arapahoe Department of Investigation could be looking for a possible Serial Killer now.

Either way, Detective Jarrett Jefferson needed to get back to the original crime scene.

As the two men decided to drive instead of walking over to see Judge Ryan Daily at the Eighteenth Judicial District building that was a Few blocks from the Sherriff's department, JJ's superior was wondering how his last piss test went.

By the way his Detective and Pete came out of the restroom that day, he seemed to have enjoyed his encounter with the Dominate Daddy's boy.

Other than his wife, No one has ever asked Mr. Jefferson if he enjoyed his sexual encounter.

Except for Randal, that was.

John was all hyped-up last year and was expecting every juicy detail about Jarrett's Special Present before Jean went missing on JJ's Birthday.

Looking over at his Chief from the passenger's side seat, JJ grabbed his crotch and gave it a tight squeeze as he professed that he still gets a Hard-On just thinking about it.

Not a response the older man was expecting.

Rob's one good opportunity to run JJ off had backfired and now there was a chance that his set up encounter to fire this man might just end up coming back and biting him in the ass.

Seeing the look of realization on Dutch's face that he just made a major screw-up, his Detective gave a slight chuckle that was followed by a calming profession from Jarrett.

Tell you what Chief; if you scratch my back, I will certainly scratch yours.

After an agreement of certain terms and conditions, both men seemed to give a sigh of relief once they realized that, "from here on out," their jobs would be safe from any and all retaliation from the other.

As the Officers pulled off South Potomac Street and into the Colorado Judicial Branch's parking lot, the pair made sure to shake each other's hand in a unanimous Let There Be Peace Agreement.

They would finally keep their noses out of each other's personal business.

CH. 6
CEASE AND DESIST.

As most days in Colorado, the warm sunshine with a high of Seventy-Six Degrees, greeted the Officers as they unbuckled and stepped out of the Department's latest acquisition. A Very Expensive Twenty Thirty Dodge Charger with a Thirty-Five Hundred Horse powered Hemi under its Mat-Black colored hood.

Chief Dutch was hoping to get one of those new-fangled flying cars, but Arapahoe County's Budget Department refused to pay the extra One Hundred Thousand Dollars for it.

The machines were still considered Highly Experimental and Way Too Costly.

Those in charge of All decisions concerning money, were not having any of the Chiefs arguments for why he So Badly Wanted something that was Completely Not Needed and Definitely Uncalled For.

But they did feel Bad for the Man; that's why a few of them got together and bought him a handheld drone for his personal enjoyment at home.

Dutch found that Unnecessary Action Rudely Unamusing and made sure they knew it too, after sending a few response pictures of the hobby vehicle crushed underneath his freshly shined work boot.

He even made sure to add the text, KISS MY ASS.

After seeing himself in the doors reflective glass, JJ Suddenly Realized that he looked like something the cat unexpectedly dragged in from its outdoor killing field of mice, birds, bugs and snakes.

Grabbing one of Jeans hair band ties he kept in his shirt's right front pocket, the first thing Mr. Jefferson did was wrap up his scraggly shoulder length hair.

He tried his best to smooth out the wrinkles from the unwashed pair of pants and long sleeve shirt pulled from his bedroom floor, but some of the stuck on dried food he had covered with them was making it almost impossible.

Thankfully, the chief just happened to have one of those Old-Time black combs that his granddad used to use.

Dutch was willing to part with it as he gave it to his Detective so that Jarrett could at least scrape most of whatever it was, off.

The travel can of Ax Body spray that was kept in JJ's left front pants pocket, shot out like a gun at the OK Corral and was used to quickly envelop the unwashed clothing that had to have sat on his bedroom floor for At Least A Week.

The chief was sure hoping JJ's appearance would not be an influence on today's outcome.

While the two overly gassed men rode the buildings elevator up to the third floor in a cloud of Lung Choking body spray, Jarrett and the Chief were now trying to decide how to label this investigation.

Without any corpses, they were still, "unofficially," dealing with just a missing persons case.

It just so happened that the missing were now numbering over Thirty.

Something that was More Than Likely going to secure JJ a search warrant now.

The only things that were upping the Ante's Importance were those skin sample slides that held an actual portion of an Officially Missing Individuals DNA. Just Where Are Their Bodies, kept being the hurdle that was slowing the Department's Investigation.

With everything they now had to consider, Both Officers were finally starting to accept the fact that Arapahoe County may have a Serial Killer working the Denver Metro area.

On top of that, what were the possibilities of there being

more storage units.

They were either looking at just the icebergs tip or this was just some sickos random, one of a kind issue.

This may be nothing more than an extreme fetish.

Either way; whoever this individual was, had pieces of an actual missing person, "and or persons," and that should not be.

As the Detective and his Supervisor strode into Judge Ryan Daily's private chambers, the two older men greeted each other as if they've been lifelong buddies. JJ was quite sure of that deduction after the judge asked Dutch how his new boy toy was working out.

The man's striking and overly feminine nephew had been wanting to join the police academy.

And after a few favors and pulling a couple of strings, Mr. Daily was able to talk Dutch into taking Pete under his wings, guidance, and firm hand.

While the pat on your back buddies were reminiscing, the next group to join their party began to stride in.

Being who they were, JJ had a suspicion that something else was in the works too.

While Jarrett was making himself comfortable, Commissioner Wess and Dina Garcia from the District Attorney's office quickly strode in before shutting the door. It seemed that not only was his current case on the docket, but so was the Detectives final evaluation on whether he would be staying with the department.

That suspicion, "after seeing the look on his Chief's face," quickly proved valid.

They were all here to discuss whether, "or not," Mr. Jefferson would be continuing his career as a Detective working for Arapahoe's Department of Internal Investigation.

The look of disgust on their faces over his personal appearance almost said everything that was needed, but thankfully Dutch stepped up to the plate before any of them had a chance to speak.

Judge, Commissioner and Miss. Garcia, currently Detective

Jarrett is leading a case that may end up becoming World Wide News.

I know that by looking at JJ and going over this past year's records of his behavior at our precinct, many, "if not most," of you would just rather end his career right now. But I'm asking you not to.

Before you pass judgment on his future, please look at what caused this Devoted Officer to slip over the edge of stability and obedience to our department.

As the panel judging group nodded their heads in agreement, Chief Rob Dutch proceeded to his evaluation of why JJ had disrespected his superiors and why he had pulled a gun on Detectives Rollins and Thomas.

Two of the Dirtiest Scumbags to have ever Disgraced the unit, according to the Chief and anyone else they might just happen to ask.

Detective Jarrett's wife Jean had went missing.

And during the investigation, Rollins and Thomas went above and beyond to set JJ up for the murder of his wife. Mr. Jefferson found out that information at the exact same time her case was going to be declared Purposely Estranged, "Not Missing," and tossed into the cold case files.

Speaking for himself, Dutch Declared there was a One Hundred Percent Chance that he would have reacted the exact same way if those Two Shit Heads had tried anything like that on either he or his family.

No Doubts About It.

Rollins and Thomas would have left his office in body bags.

Rob Dutch then went ahead to exemplify Jarrett by revealing that after the unfortunate incident, Jefferson proceeded to follow the department's disciplinary regulations to the T.

JJ never missed his Phycological Appointments, Never failed any of his drug test, "especially for alcohol," or was he ever late for work during that entire time. Since his life was turned upside down, the man was ordered to walk the tight rope of career ending death without any chances for forgiveness, to which he Professionally Mastered.

I can also tell you right now, that his current appearance has nothing to do with his recovery.

This slop of a mess is getting ready to go undercover and we are working together to successfully hide his identity just in case he comes across an everyday acquaintance. And even though JJ new this last bit of showmanship was total bullshit, he made sure to play his part as he supported the man who had his future by the balls.

He's heard through the grapevine that toy boy Pete Loves it when Daddy Dutch crushes his.

After Jarrett's Chief gave his unconditional support; the Detective was half expecting to be sent out into the hallway as they discussed his future with Arapahoe County.

Graciously, that never happened.

They didn't even interrogate him.

With the Commissioner and Miss. Garcia giving a quick yes Nod of their heads, Judge Randal then moved on to what Jarrett thought they were here for in the first place.

Tracking down a Possible Serial Killer.

With a solid pat on his back, Dutch told JJ that this is his show and it was time to move on with today's evidence surrounding this investigation.

Just what kind of corroborating materials are we looking at, the judge inquired.

Taking his time to catch his breath after that unexpected trial concerning Mr. Jefferson's life's work, Detective Jarrett started with what they found at the scene after the fire department was called to deal with a smoking containment unit at a Mile-High Storage Facility located at Twenty-Four Thousand, Four Hundred and Fifty, East Smokey Hill Road.

The crude jokes concerning just how high it was amongst those in the room, unconsciously helped the Department's Detective finally calm down a bit and relax.

Upon his arrival, the Officer found a Twelve by Eight-foot unit under full containment after the Firemen put out a window units air compressor that had started to smoke. Its motor had burnt out and appeared to be on the verge of combusting and destroying everything they now had back at their station's lab.

Thankfully, the diligence of those who ride the shiny red trucks had been able to preserve all the evidence.

After making sure the unit was secure, crime scene technicians found a barber's style chair covered in bodily fluids pertaining to sweat, spit and semen. They also inventoried Thirty-Four Light boxes that held One Thousand and Twenty skin sample slides.

At first, we didn't think there might be a case for homicide.

The DNA samples for the slides were coming back as willing participants who had either donated their bodies to science, or they had been declared legally dead by a Doctor, Coroner or Mortician.

Either way, their skin samples would have been taken and stored at locations such as Labs, Morgues or Scientific Colleges who dealt with the deceased.

Even though they are still looking at a felony crime of illegal tissue transportation, the perpetrator was more likely some sick bastard who had broken in and stolen the slides for his own disgusting pleasure.

But as of this morning, there has been a change in their investigative direction.

"So Far," Fifty of the One Thousand and Twenty slides have come back as belonging to a missing person.

There is No Way a Lab, Morgue or College, "unless they are somehow involved," should have such slides.

Also, the microscope plates all appear to be from the Eighty's.

If the evidence is correct, the skin samples are dated from January of Nineteen Eighty to December of Nineteen Eighty-Nine.

"And that's just," This Storage Unit.

It was at this point; JJ shared his suspicions that they may be looking for more than just one building.

With the buildup of bodily fluids and those appearing to be freshly deposited, this unknown individual could have been at this for over forty years now.

Not something those in the Judge's chambers wanted to hear.

While Dina Garcia readjusted herself in the awfully expensive looking leather chair, she was wanting to know if the Department had any other leads. To which JJ announced that was why they are here now.

They were needing a Cease and Desist Warrant.

Without one, the individual running the place was refusing to cooperate.

He wished they already had fingerprints to run with, but whoever used the unit was extremely careful as to not leave any. And when it came to the semen samples splattered throughout the room, his DNA wasn't in their data banks or any other state or federal systems either.

JJ even went so far as to check the data banks of all psychological and physically mental hospices that dealt with the violent and insane.

They had no traces of this individual either.

We currently have a ghost on Our Hands.

The light boxes, window unit and chair are next in the prosses of being tracked down.

The Department wasn't willing to waste time or man power until they were Absolutely Certain that an Actual Crime involving a victim had occurred.

And now they have the evidence that it has.

While the rooms officials continued to bombard the Detective with more questions, Jarrett finally started to feel something that hasn't been with him for the past year.

A sense of pride and being.

That club of I've got your back has been missing since the day Jean disappeared.

And it felt Great.

Too bad that Aura of I'm finally one of you didn't last.

The group was making plans on where they were going to have lunch, and it seemed that JJ was not invited. especially after the Chief offered to drop him off back at the Department before meeting everyone else at their chosen eating establishment.

Someplace that Most Definitely served alcohol.

The Bighorn Steakhouse.

They always kept a private room set aside just in case Judge Daily happened to show up unexpectedly.

Also, hanging with the Cool Kids was Way Below JJ's pay grade of invitation.

So, with warrant in hand, Dutch dropped off his Detective back at the unit's front door, before heading out and hanging with the cronies that oversaw what happens to an individual once they appear before the ruling party of Aristocrats.

To JJ, it was just another day in Fucking Paradise.

He Really Didn't give a shit about being invited anyway.

WHO THE HELL WANTS TO PAY TWENTY DOLLARS FOR A HAMBURGER!

Not Him.

For that price, Mr. Jefferson new of a place where he could buy Fifteen Cheeseburgers and still have enough change left over for a shamrock shake.

As the gratefulness of what just occurred concerning his job began to sink in, the widower decided to spend his lunch break doing something that he hasn't done in over a year. He was going to stop off and get some prices for his hair cut before going and buying a fresh set of clothes later that night too.

It was time to show his Chief just how much it meant to JJ when the man went to bat for his Detective and his on the rocks career.

Jarrett was fairly sure that the Stoned out of his mind hippie wasn't going anywhere.

On their first visit, the hermit looking individual appeared as if he never sets foot outside his office apartment.

While the afternoon sped towards the evening; the department's Detective who just recently had his pride restored, headed out to question his suspect, search for any new evidence and then spend the rest of his evening working to make his outward appearance match his newly found inner self who was once again able to smile.

A smile that would soon melt away like the glaciers that had once been bountiful across our wonderful planet.

He and Jean were planning to take a trip to see the last one, but life had other plans.

As JJ started his car's engine, so started that next radio advertisement AWRS was blasting across the airwaves.

At Androids With Real Skin,

If Your Lover doesn't break a sweat as you play,

Then You are having sex with A Latex Synthetic.

Why Settle For

FAKE SKIN,

When You Can Have

REAL.

Look For A

REAL SKIN DEALER

Near You.

CH. 7
WHAT'S THIS.

While Mr. Jefferson worked on dually trying to pull into Mile High's entrance with him forcibly shoving that Third Cheeseburger down his gullet, the business had that air of something was wrong.

From where the Detective was parked, JJ could see that the crime scene tape hung in tattered remains out in front of the seized unit.

From the outside, the tie-dyed drapes Mr. I Should Have Been Born In The Sixties appeared to have been ripped from their hangers. The Main entrance door to the office sat ajar and there appeared to be a spatter of blood on the doorknob.

After making sure to unholster his gun, Arapahoe's Detective very gingerly peaked through the opened entrance as he also began to shout out to anyone who may be hurt inside.

But the only voice that answered him back was Jarrett's reverberating and repeating response.

Is There Anybody In There?

Is There Anyone At Home?

That non response meant only One Thing.

It was Absolutely time to call for back up.

Especially, after stepping inside and only finding an Apocalyptic view of Total and Annihilated Destruction. The office looked as if someone was Absolutely Certain that there was something hidden within the plants.

That deduction also included every nook and cranny.

There were huge holes in the walls were either a

sledgehammer or someone's head had been shoved.

The smattering of blood made a face the likely culprit.

The plants appeared to be ripped from their pots as the pieces of the clay pottery and their bases they had been contained in, laid smashed upon the floors.

The possibility of the guy running this place leaving the now crime scene alive appeared to be slim.

But, the lack of major blood loss said otherwise.

Other than the few drops and smears of that red bodily fluid here and there, the evidence of his Hippie being murdered in the studio office seemed unlikely.

So, what happened?

Not only was there now a missing person to go along with all the others, but the computer that was listed in the warrant had disappeared also.

JJ was considering that this may have just been an unlucky robbery; but the money, other electronics and what looked like a Full Pound of Pot, sat untouched in the main part of what he would consider the apartment.

Glancing out the side window that faced the outside units, those that JJ could see still had their locks on them and undisturbed.

Even the spare keys for the storage rooms hanging on the far wall were untouched.

It was beginning to look as if the person who had the unit they were investigating, "and now this current crime scene," just might be related.

And every last fiber of his being was shouting in agreement.

Hoping that the security cameras might have caught something, Jarrett later learned that they were all fake cams.

The Very Cheap looking recorders were placed there to give a false sense of security for those few customers who might just pick their business to store some personal valuables, or the last few items pertaining to a life of misery that will soon be left unpaid for, forgotten and then sold to the Highest Bidder.

Right where his shit would have ended up being

kept, if it had not of been for the Department and his Best Friend's forceful intervention.

John showed up at JJ's door that first day of his scheduled Phycological evaluation and gave his friend no choice but to go as Mr. Jefferson was physically drug from his homestead. Randal was not taking no for an answer, to which that game lasted for the next Two Months before Jarrett finally gave in and started to go on his own.

Since the evidence he came for was no longer here, it was time to trace that air conditioner, barber's chair, and those light boxes.

These days, everything can pretty much be followed back to its point of origin.

He also wanted to see how those skin slides, dates and the missing were connected.

So far, the Detective had more questions than answers.

And the commercial playing on the offices untouched television just added to that perplexity.

This would be Jarrett's First Time to see an actual Ad from AWRS.

The company was announcing a new line of Sexual Options customers could choose from.

These Synthetics were being referred to as A Blast From The Past.

Customers could choose from a Platinum Blond Clapper from the Twenty's. A Mob Boss from the Thirty's, A Fifty's Grease Haired bad boy and they even had the Sixties covered too. You could rent a Male and Female Hippie couple that would give you the Full Woodstock Experience.

Bi, and All.

The creepy factor that sent chills up JJ's backbone, was just how identical their android was to his missing tree hugger.

He was the splitting image of that comedian called Carrot Top.

But like Jarrett's mom always said, Everyone has a twin doppelganger running around on this big blue marble.

And if you just happen to run into them, be sure to watch

your back.

Your life may just be better than theirs.

And if The Monsters realize that, their mirrored face will be the last thing you ever see before the creatures snuff you out so that they can take what you have.

JJ's Mom always referred to these things as Darkling's.

Thankfully, since the one on Television is an Android; that rabbit hole is one he doesn't have to descend.

Here at AWRS, The Past can be A Blast.

Just pick your favorite time and place,

And we will make Your Lover Everything THAT ERA Was.

If you want an Egyptian, feel his desert kissed lips against Your sweaty skin.

If a Grecian fires your desire, let her Mediterranean sand colored skin rub against Yours.

And if you want to romp naked with the liberated, meet our free loving couple from Woodstock.

They Love the feeling of skin touching skin.

Why Settle For

FAKE SKIN,

When You Can Have

REAL.

Look For A

REAL SKIN DEALER

Near You.

Just as the Departments Crime Scene Technicians started to arrive, so did Chief Dutch and Commissioner Wess.

It didn't take more than a nodding glance at each other, for the Three men to understand that the situation had just taken on an Urgency. Someone wasn't happy that Arapahoe County was interfering in their personal business.

And now, they have another missing person that is just become an unexpected part of this investigation.

It was while the Three men were discussing what was going to be their next plausible move, when one of the technicians gave a shout out.

CAPTAIN, WE FOUND SOMETHING!

Sitting on a shelf inside the kitchens refrigerator was a fresh skin sample slide with the date Zero slash Seven slash Zero slash Two slash Two slash Zero slash Three slash Zero.

The Exact Date Thomas Collins Dillon went missing.

That is also when JJ came up with the name to their culprit.

Between the skin samples and how this person likes to use the slashing symbol between the numbers, the Department's Detective decided to call this individual the Skin Slasher killer. To which Dutch and Wess Unanimously agreed.

Arapahoe Counties Finest would now be hunting someone the unit was referring to as S.S.K. or Skinner amongst those in the inner circle.

As the crime scene guys continued their latest assignment, JJ excused himself because there was other evidence that was now needing his full attention.

He had Thirty-Four light boxes, an air conditioning window unit and a barber's chair to trace.

While the Detective was trying to decide where to start, the antique barber's chair brought back a blockbuster of memories. Including those that involved JJ's dad taking his son with him as the old man went to get a haircut and shave.

Those days are long gone now.

Ninety Nine Percent of the places people go to get their hair cuts are now referred to as either Salons or Hair Stylist.

It is easier to spot a mythical unicorn these days than an actual barber shop for men.

The private moments of locker room talk, cigars and fresh razor straps are a once in a lifetime find amongst the testosterone crowd.

The chair down in Arapahoe's evidence room was Definitely a blast from the past.

What really stood out to Jarrett was its unusual design.

The red and black sitter came with a rounded instead of a squared seat cushion.

Something JJ has never seen nor had any idea they used to be designed that way.

This Rare and Antique Specimen was truly Magnificent.

The footrest heal kick plate, seat, back support, and head rest were covered in black leather with a stitched in button design.

JJ had no yearly idea when some idiot decided that it would be cost effective to remove the head rest option, but that design was something he would have loved for the companies to bring back as a comfort feature for the customer.

The fire engine red enamel frame along with the golden brass trim turned the chair into an actual work of art.

Even if he never sat in the damned thing, that chair would look great in any man cave.

Just the thought over how defiled it was as the chair served some sicko's sexual purpose, made Jarrett sick to his stomach.

He was never so grateful as to have a nice set of gloves while looking it over.

He was in need of a maker and its serial number.

Thankfully, he found both before getting to intimate with the semen crusted ass sitter.

Since this one piece of evidence might take all day, JJ decided to deal with the light boxes and air cooler at another time. He would have worked on tracking them down first, but there was a chance over a million of those pieces could have been bought by the public.

A needle in a hay stack would have been easier to find.

That chair would be more like a one of a kind treasure.

While the Detective proceeded down the internet's driveway of information, one lead after another began to pop up on the computers screen.

That Masterpiece of artisanship turned out to be made in the fifties from a company called Minerva Beauty. The chair was of the Coppola line and was considered King of The Hill when it came to Barber accessories.

It truly was the Throne of all Thrones.

Beautiful, Classy, Masculine and Comfortable: Everything, "And More," one would expect and want from a Posh barber chair.

Mr. Jefferson's day got even better once he realized that they were Not Only Still In Business, but he could pick up the phone and physically contact the company Right Now.

As he Face Timed the cute little bleached blond who was Minerva Beauty's current receptionist, JJ's Haggard appearance as a rough and tough Detective seemed to flood the gal's basement.

The information that he was asking for would not only be in the company's files; but after five minutes of searching and flirting with the long-haired officer, the exquisitely dark-skinned goddess found what he was asking for.

And that's when JJ received another unexpected surprise.

The striking woman of possible African descent with the facial structure of a western European, asked the departments detective if he would be up for a cup of coffee after a night out on the town.

Never, in Mr. Jefferson's life has he ever considered seeing a woman of color.

That self-realization also extended to the bedroom.

Something else that was never in his consideration.

The heartbreak on her face quickly showed the woman's frustration when JJ declared that he was a married man.

But it was the receptionist sigh of true disappointment which said it all, after realizing that this Extremely Hot Stud was in Colorado and she was in Monroe Georgia. It didn't help to squelch her interest in Mr. White Chocolate any less, after Jarrett denied the blonds offer of flying out to hook-up on her own personal dime and time.

He was Just That Fucking Attractive.

Jarrett's unaccepted excuse was that this case he is currently working on was taking all of his free time and there wasn't any left to play with.

Whitey also, "Once Again," reminded the striking woman that HE was Officially Married.

Do to JJ's persistence that he wasn't willing to cheat on his wife, the record keeper at Minerva Beauty gave in to the respect she felt for this man, "who was a True Keeper of the marriage vows," and offered up the only information she had concerning the last persons to have purchased and owned the cathedra.

The Coppola chair was sold to a couple by the name of John and Ruth Graves.

Adriana also let her lost catch know that she had Two different addresses for the couple.

The last home address the company had on their customers was listed as Eight, Two, Zero Seven, East Geddess Avenue. Their business The Primp and Groom Barber Shop used to be located at Three, Eight, Five, South Broadway, Englewood Colorado.

According to our records Mr. Jefferson, the Graves went out of business and shut their doors in January of Nineteen Eighty.

Once JJ realized that he had all the information available concerning the chair, he did his best to say goodbye while trying not to offend her last chance advances.

Jean would not have approved anyway.

One more Fuck Up like that on Jarrett's behalf and their marriage would Officially be over.

Mrs. Jefferson may have been willing to forgive him that first time, but there would be no second chances.

She, "PERSONALY," just happened to unexpectedly walk into their home office at Three In The Morning and found her undressed husband face chatting with a nude woman as they were both pleasuring themselves.

As the pair were smuttily discussing what they were going to do to each other in person, Jean's WHAT THE FUCK ARE YOU DOING, Quickly brought the sex show to an Instantaneous Stop.

To his wife, "even though Jarrett Swore that he has NEVER Actually screwed around on her," she considered this kind of bullshit STILL CHEETING.

That's exactly why JJ ended his call with Adriana the instant he had the information that was needed. Mr. Jefferson was afraid that Jean would have walked in and caught her Sexual Wanna Play Advances.

He'd Give Anything for that to physically happen right now.

He would also pay Anything just to hear her What The Fuck voice once again.

ANYTHING!

Just as Jarrett hung up the phone; the rabbit hole of Where Are You Jean, pulled him into its unanswerable depths.

The last things he heard before the darkness over took him was John Randal Shouting START THE CLOCK while another advertisement from Androids With Real Skin began to play.

When Your Cooking in The Bedroom,

Do You Love adding a little spice to the mix?

At AWRS, We Now Offer An S&M LINE of Dominate and Submissive Choices.

Why Settle For

FAKE SKIN,

When You Can Have

REAL.

Look For A

REAL SKIN DEALER

Near You.

CH. 8
FOLLOW THE SCENT.

As JJ's sequestered time clock clicked off the number of minutes, he was spending down the rabbit hole, the undisturbed Detective stared into the burrowed trail of mazes as it began to splinter into many outcomes and choices.

Jarrett felt as if an Eternity must have passed before he was finally able to let go of those darkened passageways that pertained to Jean.

There was something about Mr. and Mrs. Graves that seemed somehow familiar.

He just couldn't place his finger on it yet.

And those kind of intuitions always left deep scar marks in the back of JJ's brain as he continually picked at such answerable questions until they were either solved, bleeding or turning into that next wanna-be aneurism.

It usually took one of those painful and sharp grabs your attention Ghost Pains to draw him back into reality.

It was while he subconsciously started to log into the internet once again, that Tom Long, "another Detective in their department," began to shout out a set of numbers which caught JJ's startled attention.

Twelve Minutes and Thirty-Two Seconds.

No winners yet folks.

Mr. Jefferson had spaced off the fact that he had missing people and dates to find and connect also.

There were now Two choices to make, stay in the office and do desk work around these crackpots or head out and do some field work. Today just needed to be one of those times it would be best for him to just get away.

Arapahoe has a great library where the department's Detective would be able to find some peace and quiet while finishing his search for information about Mr. and Mrs. Graves.

Jarrett could also chase any rabbit hole he so wished at that time too.

He wasn't completely clueless when it came to their always deniable clock count either.

Most of Arapahoe's Investigative Department were just waiting for their fellow officer to crack.

A few had even been allowed to keep their firearms on them instead of having to check the bullet shooters in at the door like everyone else these days. Their Chief had implemented the office area as a Gun Free Zone that Very Day JJ Almost shot Rollins and Thomas.

Many years ago, during Dutch's earlier years, an officer had gone postal.

Instead of keeping his firearm in his dressing room locker like everyone else, Duke West was about to be let go for falsifying paperwork that involved one of his boys and a Driving Under the Influence charge.

He had been the one to pull his son over and was letting him go when another back up officer arrived at the scene.

Because the patrol officer felt as if Duke was feeding him a line of bullshit, the other cop just happened to see, "and remember," the plate numbers. And after comparing everything to Duke's report, Mr. Goodie Two Shoes disclosed Officer West and his Unlawful actions to Internal Affairs.

That cover-up was going to cost Duke not only his job, but his Thirty-Year Pension also.

Before Duke blew his brains out that day, "after taking down the snitch," another Three Patrolmen lost their valuable lives during that unfortunate incident too.

And now, "once Dutch was placed in charge," Department Regulations were changed, and All Officers had to check their firearms in just outside the double entrance doors which lead to the Main investigation room.

The Bio-Scanner vending machine prevented an officer's personal handgun from falling into the wrong hands and it could be locked down at any second.

Just like the double set of doors they now had to pass through.

If a firearm was detected entering through that first door, the next door would instantaneously lock while the rear door Slammed Shut and did the same. The unbreakable and bullet proof glass would act as an airtight prison cell while the culprit would be tranquilized with gas before getting restrained and removed.

The stunt JJ pulled that time in the Chiefs office was the cause for all of this must deal with now crap.

And that was another reason to get the hell out of Dodge.

His fellow Detectives were still pretty pissed over this unnecessary BULLSHIT.

It was while JJ was reaching in to retrieve his firearm that the coffin style compartment began to scratch at one of those persistent itches some Detectives with a Gut Instinct tend to get.

Mr. and Mrs. Graves were one of those prickly picking pairs.

JJ was almost positive that he has had some sort of run in with them or that last name and the nose itching scent was refusing to let go of his hound dog style tracking.

Jarrett was Absolutely One Hundred Percent Certain their involvement pertained to this case.

He would say that it was then time to pay the Graves a personal one on one visit, but that was not going to happen anytime soon.

While at the library, Arapahoe's Detective found a Denver Post article on the Graves dated January of Nineteen Eighty. The couple had been one of the First businesses to have been established in the Englewood area.

The Primp and Groom Barber Shop was closing their doors after Fifty Years of community service.

The elders who were now in their Mid Eighty's, were having an estate sale and everything inside the establishment was being auctioned off in the next few weeks.

They were hanging up their scissors.

The Front-Page Article posted a picture of the couple holding hands as they sat beside each other in two of the three chairs that were a part of the men's side of the shop.

A young man who was maybe in his late teens to his early twenties, sat in the last chair?

Jarrett couldn't find anything in the couple's interview saying just who he was.

For now, Mr. Jefferson was just going to chalk him up to either an employee, family member or fan.

There was something familiar about him; but with this picture being at least Forty Years old, there was no conceivable way the two could have ever met.

The Detective wasn't even born yet.

As the Graves record search continued, JJ learned that the barber shop was torn down years ago and its current footprint is now owned and occupied by a fast food chicken joint.

Their house was another matter.

It has been sold and resold quite a few times.

But, there was possibly a pot of gold just waiting for Detective Jefferson in their old neighborhood.

Several the houses were showing that their ownership had not been sold to strangers but were still occupied by that families next generation.

There was now a chance that someone might actually remember the couple.

Jarrett was just in the process of shutting down the library's research computer when his side radio went off.

His presence was being requested at The Mile-High Storage Units.

He was about to ask why the hell would they want him back over there, when the address Becky gave him turned out to be an entirely different one.

And that's when the pit of JJ's stomach began to bother him.

Was this going to somehow relate to his current case?

And the moment he pulled into the business's front parking lot; with his headlights bouncing off the Chief and Commissioner Wess's knowing nods, said it all.

They now had another crime scene to go with their first.

This one was slightly different, however.

It appears that One of the companies units had been broken into and compromised. Whatever had been behind that door and its three walls was long gone now.

The crime lab did find semen though.

And like the last scene, they were starting to notice the smell of cinnamon.

The studio apartment's office was just as trashed as their first attack and the computer which held the records to who was renting what from them was missing just like the last one. And even though they learned later that the security cameras were operational; the video feed went straight into the missing electronics.

Another dead end.

Well, almost that is.

There were Two skin sample slides found inside the refrigerator.

For now, they were just going to assume that it pertained to the missing employee who was supposed to be here running the business. It was later determined to be the exact match belonging to a Twenty-One-Year-old woman who went by the nickname Candy and her daughter who was only Eight.

On Zero slash Seven slash Zero slash Three slash Three slash Zero, Amber June Quinn and her daughter Zoe went missing in Arapahoe County.

The public radio announcement that was blasting over the Alexa Speaker, "before someone finally shut it off," was not helping to calm the nerves of those who were investigating this current crime scene.

AWRS's announcement seemed just a little Too Poetically

Creepy at this place and time.

There are No Better hugs and kisses than Skin on Skin.

Here at Androids With REAL SKIN

We are Now offering a Child and Young Adult Line.

If Your missing a Loved one and they've just up and vanished, You Can Now Touch Them Once Again.

Why Settle For

FAKE SKIN,

When You Can Have

REAL

Look For A

REAL SKIN DEALER

Near You.

JJ was still in the moment of processing the scene himself, when Dutch hollered for him to come outside.

By now, the Detective has also started to notice the smell of cinnamon at both scenes himself.

He had just chalked the spices overpowering smell at the Hippie's place to nothing more than incense, as the missing man was probably trying to use it to cover up that recognizable smell of pot which had permeated everything in the office.

But this crime scene was a little different.

Not only did the aroma of cinnamon drown everything in the office, but the empty storage unit out back smelled as if it had been used as a cleaner to hide whatever they were missing.

For now though, JJ would have to dwell on that later; he was once again being called outside.

His Chief and the Commissioner needed to talk with him.

They were interested in Jefferson's current thoughts and were wondering if there have been any new leads in this case.

His answer was a welcomed surprise.

Jarrett was able to track the barber's chair to a couple by the name of Graves.

Even though they are no longer alive, the belongings that had been a part of the business were then sold in a mass buy off by Rothchild Estate sales.

He will be looking into them tomorrow.

Mr. Jefferson also had the couples old address and would be canvassing that area for any of their old friends or acquaintances who may just happen to still be in the area too.

The last of their DNA evidence from the skin samples should be arriving any day now.

And once that happens, the Detective would finally be able to see how the dates that were associated with the slides added up.

That coalition would eventually show that the found skin sample was taken and dated THE EXACT DAY that individual was declared missing. The few that were off, ended up being reassigned after seeing that the families had tried reporting their missing loved one's days earlier than what was documented.

The Department now had an Accurate date for when that person actually went missing.

It also gave most of the cold cases another reason to be reopened.

New and Untapped Evidence.

Finishing up the conversation, the men were about to head their separate ways when an unknown male tried to approach the taped off crime scene.

He was Demanding to talk with Whoever was in charge.

The gentleman who appeared to be in his Golden Years, just so happened to own every Mile-High Storage facility in the state.

Now that Two of his businesses were under investigation, he was afraid of losing both locations. He was also working on saving face with those customers who were being kept from their personal belongings.

Just call me Bart was willing to help and do whatever it took to get his units up and running again.

After sharing what was going on; without compromising their evidence, Detective Jarrett explained what they were needing. The department was wanting to know just who rented this and the other unit that was now part of a duel crime scene.

The revelation about what was occurring, seemed to shock

the older man into action.

Once he gets back home, Bart said that he was More Than Willing to help and would send them any and everything he had concerning the Bio-Hazzard rooms

The owners unexpected visit would eventually bring Arapahoe's Investigative Department a partial break that would eventually help solve the cases.

It seemed that the missing computers not only had a name, address and phone number attached to them, but that information was kept and compiled at the owner's personal residence.

The clues were starting to mount up and Arapahoe's Chief of Police, Commissioner and JJ couldn't have been any happier.

S.S.K's trail was getting warmer and warmer.

The person nick named Skinner was now in the bull's eye of JJ and the department.

And their Killer knew it too.

That old ass air conditioner he's been meaning to replace, finally costed him a decade's worth of trophies.

Due to its faulty compressor, thousands of dollars' worth of light boxes had been taken for evidence. One of his favorite chairs had also been seized during the fire departments illegal entry into HIS SANCTUARY.

The Eighty's room of skin samples had also been the largest part of his collection.

And now they were gone.

ALL GONE!

Thankfully, he decided to try and be one step ahead of the police before they accidently stumbled upon his collection of memorabilia from the Nineties.

That was also the decade where he Officially decided to prepare and take his skin samples from the living instead of the dead. The Killer needed to do this because the morgue where he worked and the lab that S.S.K. ran deliveries for, were starting to get suspicious.

It seemed that Skinner had been overly handsy during that

time.

Yes, samples do get mislabeled or accidently go missing now and then; but that rare and unusual mishap started to become One To Many for the administrations Skinner worked for. Especially the Infectious Disease labs who dealt with Extreme and Deadly Viruses amongst the population.

It was Skinner's unexpected firing that finally sent him down the path Arapahoe's Finest were now having to deal with.

And what they are currently dealing with, was just the tip of S.S.K's iceberg.

CH. 9
SKINNER.

As the collector stood back and did his best to blend in with the growing crowd, the killer was close enough to hear the Detective agree to meet the owner at his house first thing tomorrow morning.

He also caught the fact that every file concerning Mile High Storage Units was kept at a main frame.

Also at the man called Bart's house.

The unsuspecting observer realized that if he could snatch that computer before the cops got to it, he would then have enough time to empty out all of his other trophy cases.

Doing his best not to draw any unwanted attention, Arapahoe's first ever Serial Killer began to stalk his next victim. The gentleman who referred to himself as Bart quickly headed back to his car: He was in a hurry to return home so that he could copy the information the cops were needing.

Everyday any one of his businesses were down, was costing him thousands in untapped rentals.

Something he was Not Willing to accept.

It was while getting into his vehicle, the business owner noticed that he may have gotten some unwanted attention. A gentleman a bit older than himself was paying a little more scrutiny to him and his vehicle than he was willing to accept.

The bald man who appeared to be Well Over Six-Foot-Tall, was paying attention to every move that Bart was making.

As the possible stalker disappeared into the crowd, Mile-High's owner felt a bit of relief as he pulled West onto East

Arapahoe Road before heading North onto South Buckley Road with no trace of the man in his rearview mirror.

It wasn't until Bart turned Right onto East Wagontrail Parkway that he started to become spooked.

A few cars behind him was a bald man in the driver's seat of another vehicle.

The older man thought that it Might be the same person, but the afternoon sun blinded his line of sight as he looked into the vehicle's rearview mirror.

And that's when Bart decided Not to take any chances.

In the past, Bart's wife had to take a mandatory defensive driving class after almost taking out an entire group of adults and kids as they were strolling through a cross walk.

She was on her cell phone and didn't see the flashing warning sign.

Thank God she didn't kill anyone that day.

During her class, they both learned that women were Sixty Percent more likely to be followed and stalked than men.

For the Elderly, that possibility shot up to Eighty Percent.

It was explained that the easiest way to catch such a person as that, was to immediately make FOUR Right Hand Turns. The explanation for that reaction was due to the fact that no one in their right mind has a need to make That Many Right Turns.

If that scenario were to happen, it was just safer to head for the nearest police station or a Very Public venue.

Stalkers, kidnappers and Murders Hate areas that will expose their illicit plans.

Remembering everything his wife had been taught, Bart proceeded to follow the instructors advice.

Thankfully, those Four right turns he took by himself, quickly settled his frayed nerves.

No one was following him.

The thing that was unknown to Bart, was that his stalker had taken those same defensive driving classes himself.

Once S.S.K. realized what his prey was doing, Skinner just parked his vehicle and waited for the startled man to complete his driving around the block escape plan. And after Bart wrapped up his Four corner turn, Skinner held back a little father this time and finished following the man back to his private residence.

As Bart Pulled into his home address at Seventeen Thousand, Five Hundred and Fifty-Nine East Temple Drive, his only mission at that time was to grab a Memory Stick and download all the information that the Detective would be needing.

He also wanted to do this because the fear of being followed was still nagging at him.

The car that drove past his house, "just as he was walking in the front door," sort of looked like the one he had seen earlier.

That hinting gut suspicion saying he has been followed would turn out a little later to be true.

Running into his house and getting his entire business dealings downloaded onto a memory stick, Bart was able to get it addressed and into an envelope just as the pick-up and delivery company he called, "before leaving the latest incident at one of their facilities," was walking up to his front door.

It was while assuring his wife her winded husband was more than okay, that Bart just happened to catch a similar car drive back by their location in his peripheral vision.

But, with everything happening at that moment; the business owner just couldn't be sure.

Unlike his future prey, Skinner was Absolutely certain of a few things.

After nightfall, he was getting into that house and taking his next victims' computer. He would also take any and every last record of the man's business dealings.

And then he would do as he always does.

S.S.K. would once again add to his skin collection.

As the stalker headed out to grab the supplies that would be needed for tonight, his FAVORITE Company began to play one of their Commercials.

We here at AWRS, we know the hardship of missing an elderly Loved One.

That's Why, we now offer a Later In Life line.

YOU can now, "ONCE AGAIN," Feel the touch of a Parent or Grandparent.

And Nothing sooths that pain MORE, than Skin against Skin.

Why Settle For
FAKE SKIN,
When You Can Have
REAL.
Look For A
REAL SKIN DEALER
Near You.

As Bart's stalker considered heading back to where the Serial Killer's main operation was kept, his love for AWRS was a Major part of his life and the plastered walls with their adds inside Skinner's vehicle said everything one would want to know about the man.

They had his Full Support.

At least Once A Week, S.S.K. walked through their doors and spent time with the employees and their synthetic beings. And ever since their REAL SKIN line went into production, Skinner surprisingly ended up becoming one of the business's main suppliers.

The man LOVED and DESIRED the feel of REAL SKIN.

For tonight though, Bart's huntsman had noticed that this evening was going to be a Two for One deal.

Kind of like the mother and her little girl.

The owner's wife just happened to be approaching their front door as he drove back by one last time.

As Skinner turned east onto Quincy Avenue, his heart began to pace while his pulse quickened. He was getting excited over the thought that tonight two adults would be getting skinned.

His little warehouse of Horror's sat just off Bennett Road.

About Five miles west of County Road Fifty-Three sat an unassuming dirt road that leads to a rundown building sitting about Half a Mile south of Quincy.

The chamber Skinner did his business in couldn't have been any larger than a Thousand Square Feet or so. Small enough that most motorist never took notice of the rambled shack like structure as they sped their way past it.

But that apple of his eye shines brighter than the sun when he first spots it.

And even though he now has to deal with a diagnosis of Erectile Disfunction in his old age, being here always gives S.S.K. a semi-hard on. Tonight, was going to be a busy one and he had to make sure that everything was cleaned, prepped and ready to go.

The skin clamps needed to be inspected for any defaults that may have occurred during his last skinning, the Spiced Brine had to be checked for balance and flavor and the butchery equipment was in dire straits of sanitation if tomorrows ground round processing was to be delivered on time.

He found the willful spreading of Salmonella, UNACCEPTABLE.

Especially By Other Butchers.

Skinner would have you ask Willey over at Whiles' Market about having that issue and blaming it on S.S.K's place of business, but the Daily Special that acquired his involvement was sold out over Two Weeks ago.

He was also needing to put the cage back into its rightful place.

Just feet from the slaughter table.

The Butcher had moved it so the little girl wouldn't have to see up close just what he was going to do with her mother before she herself ended up on the skinning slab.

S.S.K. had tried leaving a snot noser in place once, as he worked on the kid's parent; but The Little Shit THROWER caused him to fuck up the Dad's skin and that mistake costed him a business loss of somewhere in the Tens of Thousands range.

After his refusal to Shut The Fuck Up Fiasco, the boy's Earth-Shattering SCREAMS were quite pleasurable while his torturer took his sweet time on the little tyke.

The little girl last night was a different story, she just whimpered and cried.

Those tears of I'm So Sorry and I will Do Whatever You Want, still brings a smile of contentment to the lips of their unnamed killer.

This night however, Skinner was going to make the wife watch as he Deskins the businessman first. S.S.K. was wondering just what the old woman would be willing to say and do just to protect her unsavable husband.

And that future scenario began to play out a little after Eight P.M. that night.

After forcing his way into their home under the guise that he had walked away from his senior living center and was now lost and in need of a phone, S.S.K. was able to get a choke hold on his victim while knocking the storage owner out with the saturated cloth of Ether being pressed into his face.

Mrs. Bartholomew never knew what hit her either.

She no sooner stepped around the corner to see what all the fuss was about, when their home invader laid her out with a Firing Stun Gun of Fifty Thousand Volts.

Neither had any memory of what took place next as Arapahoe's Killer began to strip the house and its home office of all computers, laptops and any other devices that might hold information concerning Mile High Storage.

The perpetrator even went so far as to take every last piece of paper that was kept in the office's filing cabinets.

The last thing S.S.K. did was to make sure and leave his calling card.

Skinner placed Two skin sample slides in the couples refrigerator dated, Zero slash Seven slash Zero slash Four slash Three slash Zero.

He also did something with this crime scene that had not been done to the others.

S.S.K. left a blank sample slide with the initials JJ where the skin should have been.

Skinner was hoping that the Detective might be up for a

game of cat and mouse.

Finishing with what was needed for the fourth crime scene that will be associated to him, the home invader did one last Ether check on the Bartholomew's before it was time to head out.

He did not want them to wake up until it was time.

And that timing needed to be perfect.

Bart's wife was the first to awaken while finding herself handcuffed to the ice-cold floor of a steel prison. It was the woman's Demand to Let Her Out Of This Cage as she begged to know What He Was Doing To Her Husband, which caught Bart's drug induced attention.

Mr. Bartholomew was laying on his face while being sprawled out in a hanging on the cross pattern.

The semi-conscious man was under the influence of opium that had been administered directly into his veins about Twenty Minutes earlier.

Everything felt as if it was cream and butter.

This feeling of Euphoria was intoxicating to him.

And even though he couldn't focus on anything in his drugged-up stupor, the victim could tell that his attacker was in the process of doing something to the backside of his body.

After being shaved from the top of his head to the bottom of his feet, S.S.K. had scalpel in hand and was in the process of making his first slits in the skin. And even though Mile High's owner couldn't feel anything, he was able to hear the zipper like sound as his flesh began to separate.

That first cut ran from the center of Bart's forehead; back over the skull and all the way down his back, right to where the backbone met the pelvis.

The second cut started out on the back of the victim's left hand, "right at the index finger's base," and then proceeded up the arm, across the back and then over to his right hand.

Stopping at the exact same place as on the left.

The third and fourth cuts went from the lower back, "starting where the first cut stopped," and down each leg.

The killer's scalpel didn't stop its incision until curving

around the heal and splicing right up to the foots middle toe.

And even though Bart was in some sort of drug induced limbo; the SCREAMS, SCREAMING from his SCREAMINGLY SCREAMING wife, SCREAMED SCREAMINGLY all that was needing to be SCREAMINGLY SCREAMED.

This animal was skinning him alive and it seemed that The Monster was finding Enjoyable Pleasure in the process. Mr. Bartholomew chalked that revelation up to the fact that his perpetrator was sucking on some kind of cinnamon snack while he was getting everything ready for Bart's next procedure.

The unknown assailant was also playing a song by some Musical Group called Marmaduke Duke.

Skin The Mother Fucker Alive.

Quite befitting for this moment, Bart thought to himself.

S.S.K's little Feeling The Spirit Dance Shuffle as he clicked his butcher knives together, seemed to be feeling the exact same way.

Before flipping his victim over, Skinner took clamps and placed them along both sides of the spliced skin. Making sure they were all securely locked in place, the attached chains that had been turned One Hundred and Eighty Degrees began to lift Bart into the air.

The older gentleman was able to observe that the table top he had been laying on was nothing more than a container lid covering the butcher's next batch of brining liquid.

As his captor flipped him a Full One Hundred and Eighty Degrees; so that the chains returned to their proper positioning, the storage facilities owner now found himself facing the structure's interior roof.

That's also when the clamped victims weight began to pull the skin apart from those last vestiges of collagen which kept it affixed to the muscle.

All the while; the electric motors attached to the metal links continued to lift him towards the buildings pitted tin ceiling.

The revelation that what might be happening next was hard to comprehend due to the fact that all Bart could hear at this moment was his skin separating from the body.

That, and his SCREAMING wife as she awoke from her fainting spell.

Just as his misses rose from the floor, Mrs. Bartholomew looked up just in time to see her husband fall as if he was partaking of the weirdest bungee jump ever.

When the chains snapped to an instantaneous stop just above the water line, she Horrifyingly watched Bart's Entire Body deglove itself from his muscled frame. What was left of his now unskinned self, fell into the vat of liquid below it.

The last thing she remembers seeing before ending up on the table herself, was her husband's skin dangling in the air while Bart turned to give her one last look from his watery grave.

While his second victim was awaiting her turn, "and since she wasn't going anywhere any time soon," Skinner started on tomorrow's ground chuck order.

It was his Boisterous Humor which caught the trapped woman's attention.

Her attacker was Laughingly referring to something as more like Fresh Ground Bart.

Being the inquisitive woman that she was, Beth just had to ask.

What was that?

It wasn't until he turned around to answer the woman's question, that her SCREAMS erupted once again. The man who had been standing with his back to her, now faced his captive with a butchered forearm in his hand.

Skinner was feeding a portion of her husband into a meat grinder.

From the look of how full the tub laying at his feet was, Most of Bart had already been processed.

Hanging just around an unseen corner from her earlier advantage, were racks of sausage and sweet breads that were being dried and preserved for later consumption. They were either about to go in or had just been pulled from the smoker.

There attached to one of the walls, "amongst Hundreds of

AWRS posters," was a business sign.

Graves Butchery and Meat Market.

"Not Only!" was THAT; THE EXACT MARKET her and her family have been shopping at for close to Twenty Years Now, but enough of the Ether and former shock had worn off so that the victim could finally make out her attacker.

It was Bill Graves.

He's The Owner of Graves Deli and a Very Good Friend of Theirs who sits next to the Jewish Couple at their Synagogue during services honoring the Sabbath.

Mrs. Bartholomew just couldn't believe what she was seeing and hoped that this was all just a drug induced hallucination. She's had medications do that to her in the past. Especially when the chemotherapy sessions started.

Those were some Alice In Wonderland Days.

"AND," she did start a new regiment of pills just a few weeks ago.

It wasn't until Mr. Graves turned around and began to speak, that his captive started to realize that this was no dream.

It Was An ACTUAL, LIVING, NIGHTMARE.

As she began to sink into euphoria from the fresh morphine filled syringe, Graves was asking his SCREAMING victim if she was ready to join her husband as part of tomorrows daily specials.

Ground Bart and Beth Bartholomew would be selling for Fifty Cents a pound.

Graves would also be making his Famous Meat Pies.

And that's when Beth's Horror OVERROAD the drug's effects.

The SCREAMS that exploded from the depths of her core came from a shocking revelation; Mr. Graves's Kosher Meat Pies were served Every Sabbath at her house.

It was the next realization which caused her Uncontrollable SCREAMS to echo their symphonic masterpiece within the shed. Beth's sister' June, was scheduled to pick up the Meat Pies tomorrow.

Skinner loved it when his victims SCREAMED.

Today, Beth's SCREAMS would go down in his record books as the best ones yet.

Her Tear Choking SCREAMS touched Skinner's Blackened Soul as No others ever have.

They Moved Him.

CH. 10
CAT AND MOUSE.

Since the last few days have ended up being a handful, Detective Jarrett was looking forward to doing some on-hands footwork. He was going to head over to Eight, Two, Zero Seven, East Geddess Avenue and see if anyone in the neighborhood was still around after the Graves used to live there.

Several the houses surrounding theirs were still listed as either the same owner or passed on to that next family member.

And JJ's suspicion soon payed off.

Quite a few of the elderly people remembered John and Ruth Graves.

According to most, if you were ever in need, the couple would give you the shirts off their backs. They even went so far as to gift free haircuts to the housebound and those who did not have money and looking for a job.

It was such a sad day when the Graves were left with no choice but to sell their business.

The Couple wanted to keep it in the family, but that Weird Ass Son of theirs wanted nothing to do with hair.

That boy was nothing but a Total failure and Disappointment to his parents.

While a few more neighbors shared their thoughts and opinions about the Graves, Mr. Jefferson was starting to wonder just why he couldn't find anything related to a son. It seems any and everything pertaining to the young man had somehow been stricken from the records.

The unnamed kid just Magically up and vanished one day.

Sadly, anyone who could have known and played with the young Graves had moved from the neighborhood long ago.

Arapahoe's Detective came across another dead end later that day after tracking down the company who handled the Businesses' liquidation. Ago.

Their investigation turned out to be a Blatant case of arson.

The Owners and Insurance Investigators were blaming either the family, a disgruntled employee, or a ripped off seller.

It turned out that Rothchild Estates had more than One criminal case filed against them.

The Company was well known for screwing customers while physically threatening to violently harm the seller if they did not keep their God Damned Mouths Shut.

It wasn't long after that, Mr. Rothschild and his wife went missing.

Their oldest son, "who carried out the violence," also went missing about a year later.

As Jarrett climbed back into his Dodge Charger, the name Graves really started to press on his I Know This Name Button.

He's heard it before, but JJ just couldn't seem to settle on a time or place.

Jefferson was hoping Mr. Bartholomew would have called him by now with the information that was needed, but there's been no luck in that department just yet. So, to occupy sometime, Jarrett went back to his office at the Department and began to sort through the names and dates of all the skin sample slides.

It was while going over the DNA results that a mystery lasting over the past Forty-Five Years was partially solved.

Three of the samples came back as Mr. and Mrs. Rothschild and their missing son Danny.

Seems the family had a run in with S.S.K. and he was now responsible for taking All of their lives.

Whoever it was that had purchased the chair from John and

Ruth's going out of business sale, understood that their records would hold that kind of information. Just as any and all Rothschilds and family members who had been a part of the sale would have known about those files too.

That's a sure bet as to why S.S.K. took them.

They knew exactly who the person was and what the individual looked like.

While lunch time was in the prosses of rolling into early afternoon, JJ received an unexpected call from Dutch.

The Chief was needing Jarrett to meet him at Seventeen Thousand, Five Hundred and Fifty-Nine, East Temple Drive.

Once More, Skinner has struck and there seems to be Two missing victims again.

Their mystery person also left a little surprise for JJ.

Seems the Detective has a Star Struck Fan now.

It was while Jefferson stopped off at the vending machine to retrieve his gun, that the Chief ended his call with a harsh reality.

The missing couple are the ones who own the Mile-High storage units.

A Mr. and Mrs. Bart and Beth Bartholomew

And by the way, there's an empty slide with your initials.

Not only did that last bit of information floor JJ, his reaction to that shocking revelation sent Jarrett's foot flooring that Dodge Charger's pedal to the metal in response.

Arapahoe's first ever Serial Killer now had a body count that was somewhere in the hundreds to possibly thousands now. They really had no idea what was in that second storage unit or how many more skin sample slides it may have held.

The one thing that JJ could say for sure was S.S.K, "in the last Five Days," has added another Five People who are now on the declared missing list.

However, many more that would turn out to be, all depended on just how quickly JJ and the Department moved in their investigation. Without a name to go with Skinner, the likelihood of them catching this person would have been almost impossible.

But JJ had unintentionally caught the killer's attention.

S.S.K. was not going anywhere.

Neither was the package that was sitting on Jarrett's desk once he got back to the office.

Going over the crime scene, it seemed that whoever had taken the couple had also stolen the computer and all electronics that might have had the information also.

Even the filing cabinets were missing.

This Crime location also presented a unique piece of evidence that matched the other Two scenes, the air inside Bartholomew's house smelled Just Like Cinnamon.

It was so strong, that the attacker either carried straight cinnamon oil with them or they had a thing for atomic fireballs or those little red hots. JJ only came to that conclusion after searching the house for anything else that could be perpetrating such an unusual scent.

And like All the other crime scenes, the missing had nothing on the premises that had such aromatic qualities.

They now had to add the scent of cinnamon to the list of unexplained coincidences.

As the Two Men began to bounce ideas and possibilities off each other, the department's dispatcher Becky was trying to get a hold of Jefferson.

The postal service just dropped off a package for him.

It was stamped URGENT.

As she began to apologize to JJ for going against his wishes and contacting him at an active crime scene, the Very Young Miss Grove timidly announced that he needed to immediately return to the station

There was a small envelope addressed to him from a Mr. Bartholomew.

And since this name seemed to match their latest victim, she thought it of Utmost Importance.

The department's Detective couldn't believe his luck.

Had the Old Coot gone home and decided to send him the information in advance.

That question was immediately answered the moment JJ

plugged in the Flash Player.

Mr. Bartholomew had left him a message and what to look for. Before announcing what he found, the now missing man shared with the Detective that he felt as if he had been followed after talking with him earlier.

Stating that he wasn't really sure if he had seen something or if it was just nerves, Bart recollected the fact he thought that a very tall and good-sized bald man had been trailing him from the storage units.

He felt this was worth saying because a car like the one which followed him earlier had driven back by the house.

TWICE.

Being an idiot when it came to identifying vehicles, Bart could only recollect that it was Red and had Two Front Doors plus a Double Set of Back Doors. The windows for the backdoors were almost unrecognizable do to all the dirt.

"The thing is," it wasn't anything like the current van shapes we observe on the road these days.

It kind of had a retro design like the one's people see in old surfer movies such as in the beach boy era. The vehicle was also really dirty and looked as if there had been a sign on its side, or one that had recently been removed.

As Bart apologized for not knowing more, there was something he could tell and show the Detective.

The phone number related to the Two units was the same: The name given was not.

Also, that number was attached to another Three Units.

The next phone call that arrived at Jarrett's desk quickly cut that count down to Two units.

Another Mile-High Storage facility has just been robbed.

And those who oversaw the place, are now missing.

With another Two Crime scenes in their future, JJ was fixing to send more officers to those locations when his We Got This Smile instantaneously dissipated into a Defeating Frown.

It seems that Bart was in such a frazzled Hurry, he downloaded the incorrect information.

There would be no preemptive strike as JJ was hoping for.

In Arapahoe County, Mr. Bartholomew owned Thirty Storage facilities.

The man also had Well Over Two Hundred just in the surrounding Denver Metro.

And Who's to say that S.S.K. only used his.

According to his internet search, just in their area of the front range were Over One Thousand businesses offering a place to store a person's personal goods. And if each facility offered One Hundred choices to choose from, the department would now be looking at having to apply for almost One Hundred Thousand search warrants.

This setback was definitely going to not only cost the investigation some valuable time; but if Skinner decided to step out of the county, their department would be Truly Fucked.

It's Never a good thing when other Investigative Offices and Counties have to become involved.

Not Only does the Fact Finding turn into a Shit Show, but you now have other Gung Ho Detectives trying to steal your thunder and collar.

Not something Jarrett, his Chief or Commissioner was wanting to happen.

Since All Mile-High Units carry the same floor plan, the crime scenes were literally a carbon copy of each other.

This location was ran by a Lesbian couple who were Bi-racial.

The African American woman and her Asian girlfriend were last seen yesterday afternoon. The gentleman who had rented his unit at the last moment, had decided to return bright and early due to his credit card being overcharged by One Hundred Dollars.

He said that when he arrived, his anger was just wanting to kick down the front door to the office / studio apartment and surprise the gals in hopes of getting his money back.

But once here, he didn't need to.

The door was already opened.

Seeing the condition of the demolished room and knowing that he was the last person they saw, "also understanding that he was here before anyone else," would make him suspect Numeral Uno.

That is why he instantaneously called the Police.

The company's latest customer desired no part of whatever happened here.

After finishing with his statement, JJ wanted to know if he had seen anything or anyone else on the premises that night. At which the witness pointed to the opened unit out back that was currently being processed for evidence.

Yes, he proclaimed.

There was a guy loading some kind of boxes into a weirdly shaped truck or maybe it could have been a van.

With all of the exterior lights out down that driveway's portion, it was impossible to get a really good look at him or exactly what he was doing. Anyway, I did my best not to stare because I considered what the man was trying to achieve as none of my personal business.

He did look up once and actually caught me glancing at him.

That's the other reason I stopped paying attention.

After His verbal response of What The Fuck, I thought it best just to mind my own business.

As JJ was dismissing his witness, the guys who were assessing this current location Hollard out that the strong scent of cinnamon has officially been detected at both the office and empty storage unit.

There was something in the apartment that Jarrett needed to see also.

The Detective was just about to walk into the office when his witness gave a waving honk of his vehicle as he drove off. If Jefferson had stayed outside a little longer to watch the young man leave, he might have noticed the Nineteen Fifty-Three Grungy Red Panel Truck, "with no side windows," that seemed to hold back as it followed the Detective's witness from the area.

But the Loud, Get In Here Quick SHOUT from inside, needed his Undivided Attention.

The Crime Technicians found more skin sample slides.

Due to the assorted colors of flesh between the pieces of microscope glass, it looked as if the samples belonged to the missing couple. S.S.K. had struck again and on Zero slash Seven slash Zero slash Five slash Three slash Zero, Ti Cabell and Aniqua Brown were declared missing.

The third had no sample at all.

Just the initials JJ.

The slide also contained the numbers Three slash Zero.

It wouldn't be until months down the road before the Investigative Department found out that their witness had been declared missing that following morning.

His skin sample was eventually added to the list of victims brought down by Skinners hands.

Johnny Sims.

Zero slash Seven slash Zero slash Six slash Three slash Zero.

Because the young man was from a different state and his presence had only been in the area for less than a week, no one, "other than his family back in Virginia," had reported him missing.

Like most Non-Native Coloradans, he just fell off the radar.

For years afterwards, what actually happened to his body would remain an unspoken mystery. Arapahoe's Department of investigation just couldn't bring themselves to tell his family were his hamburger ground remains ended up.

Somewhere between Graves butcher shop, his meaty donations to Denver's homeless shelters and the Toilet Shitter.

CH. 11
WHAT'S NEXT.

As Day Seven of Jarrett's investigation began, having a day off had done wonders for the Detective.

With all that was taking place, his mind had been occupied enough that Jean had been far from his thoughts. She didn't stick her nose into his business until waking up yesterday and realizing that he had forgotten about his promise to go clothes shopping.

But, before he was willing to do that; JJ bent over and began to pick up his plague infested house.

Just the pile of dirty clothes laying in front of his soon to be Overly worked washing machine, stood At Least Three feet tall by Five Feet Wide. The smell emanating from all the fabrics would have made a Perfect Bomb for chemical warfare.

That Bio-Hazzard cleanup revealed hundreds of dry and encrusted land mines.

His Very First plate of food that had been thrown the day Jean went missing was still visible.

JJ was itching to run the wet vacuum cleaner over the carpet, but there was still a years' worth of trash to deal with.

And that was just downstairs.

Between the upstairs, down stairs and what was piling up in the garage; one of those massive dumpsters you see at a construction site would be needed to hall off this garbage dump.

Mr. Jefferson was So Grateful that he was living far enough up north that Roaches were a Rarity. If this house had been down south in more of a tropical atmosphere, the Two-Story structure would have needed one of those fumigating tents.

He ABSOLUTILY Did Not Miss turning on the lights while trying to get a midnight drink of water and seeing the entire floor move out of your foot stepping way.

And even though you may have washed your dishes squeaky clean, the house rule was to always rewash any and everything you plan to drink and eat from. You even needed to check every last piece of enclosed food that had been left out.

More than once, Jarrett went to grab a piece of bread and the roaches had already eaten a hole through the plastic before beginning their already packed roach motel within the bag.

That's why most Northerners don't understand why bread is kept refrigerated down south.

Roaches and the fact that bread tends to mold overnight if kept out in a warm and humid climate, are great reasons to do so, if you want to eat a safe and uncontaminated sandwich ever again.

Those little bastards can even squeeze their way into an Air Tight Sealed box of Cereal or Pasta.

While his clean up continued, Mr. Jefferson was quite surprised to see that there were no rats or droppings during his decontamination of their house.

Jean would have been proud.

As his day off began to pass, the widower had no sense of time until his stomach began to growl its empty unhappiness.

It was just past One in the afternoon.

Jean's from the grave guilt has had her husband on his feet for the last Seven Hours.

And the improvement was Spectacular.

His next move would have had Mrs. Jefferson clawing for his sexual attention.

Jarrett was headed out to get his hair cut and to also purchase a new wardrobe so that he would finally look like the clean-cut stud she had married.

JJ missed that lustful look on Jeans face when he would

walk out of their bathroom just wearing his Officers cap and nothing else but the accessories belt, baton, cuffs, and leather boots that complimented the uniform.

Just remembering how she would rub her hands over his rock-hard chest and washboard abdominal muscles, was creating a Sexual response that JJ hasn't felt in a Very Long time.

And that's when her, **I MISS YOU TEARS,** began to roll down her husband's cheeks.

If Jean were to see the condition her widowed husband was currently in; it would have crushed the woman's soul.

There was No Need for him to have caused such personal and self-inflicting damage to himself.

Mrs. Jefferson knew that JJ Loved her, but if she were here right now; his missing wife would have finally accepted the fact that he Actually **DID** think of her as his Soul Mate.

Now that its officially been over a year, the Department's Detective decided that it was time to pick up his crushed spirit and begin the process of moving on.

Since that first batch of wash had finished its run in their dryer, the haggard house cleaner in him began to kick his ass into that next gear. It was time to take a shower, iron some clothes before getting dressed and then he was expected to go out and Actually spend some money on his own self-improvement.

Not even One Mile from the Detective's house sat an outdoor mall, theater, several clothing outlets, and some Great Places to eat.

Chilies was Mr. Jefferson's Ultimate Go Too.

And since it was already going on Two in the afternoon, JJ's lack of energy levels was telling him that it was time to get something to eat.

Switching out the loads in the washroom, before heading out; the house phone did something it hasn't done in like forever.

It rang.

Someone was actually calling him at home.

Picking up the receiver and offering his go-to phrase, "Jefferson Residents," Dutch quickly responded back with, how's it going JJ.

The Chief was just checking in to see how he was handling everything.

Being that time of the year, the Supervisor wanted to make sure his Investigator wasn't starting to crack under all the pressure of dealing with not only a Possible Serial Killer, but also having to work with people who have now been declared missing like his wife was.

Dutch understood that not only was this case hitting close to Jarrett's home, it was physically trying to crawl into the lap of his Lead Detective.

He needed Mr. Jefferson to be in Tip Top shape because when it came to investigations that were trickier than a Chinese puzzle box, Jarrett was his best problem solver. Besides that, He's become quite attached to the man after everything his Officer has went through and survived.

It didn't hurt that what happened between him and Pete in the bathroom; was something that Dutch, "as their future workplace endeavors allowed their paths to unquestionably cross," hoped to repeat.

But this time, he was going to try and make it a Three-some.

Something Officer Kunkle just couldn't seem to let go of, as he begged for Daddy Dutch's permission to once again play with the man who gives Golden Showers.

As the Two Men made small talk, JJ was starting to get anxious.

This was his only day off and he still had an extensive list of chores that were needing to be accomplished.

The biggest one was getting his hair cut and having his beard removed.

The only thing staying would be the requested handle bar cut that always Kettle whistled Jean's Tea Pot.

Once that hat was applied with his dark sunglasses, Mr. I'll Take What I Want Bad Boy could have and do anything he wanted or demanded. She was his suspect and Officer

Jefferson could interrogate her ANYWAY HE DAM WELL PLEASED.

As the rest of Dutch's conversation began to fall on deaf ears do to the fantasy that was playing out in Jarrett's head, a red panel van slowly drove by the widow JJ was day dreamily looking out of.

And due to the depth of that rabbit hole, what he just saw went right over his head.

It wasn't until the Chief started to shout at his Detective, that the widower snapped back into reality.

Dutch was trying to apologize for bothering him on his day off, but he just wanted to give JJ a heads up concerning a few more pieces of evidence that just arrived this afternoon concerning the skin slide identification of those who were, "or where not," declared missing.

Two of the samples came back as John and Ruth Graves.

Both identification dates were listed as Zero slash Three slash Two slash One slash Eight slash Zero.

It seems that even though they were never declared missing, they appear to have had a run in with Skinner Two Months after selling the business. And, we might have a break in the case concerning who their estate Wasn't left too.

A man by the name of Bill Graves.

It seems that they Actually Had a Son.

Taking that as his Cue to get off the phone, Jarrett told Dutch that their disappearance would be one of the First things he would be looking into tomorrow morning.

After explaining to the Chief exactly why he was in such a hurry to let him go, Dutch's responding answer was ABOUT FUCKING TIME. That conversation ender also costed JJ to miss the vehicle that drove back by as he turned to hang up the phone.

A Red, Nineteen Fifty-Three Dodge Panel Truck with no side windows and Desperately In Need of a bath.

If JJ had been looking closely, the faded businesses name could Almost be made out under all the mud and dirt and would have Most Certainly caught the Detectives attention.

Graves Meat Market and Deli.

As Mr. Jefferson sprinted out his front door, JJ couldn't remember the last time he has ever felt this Exhilarated to get a haircut and a Fresh New Pair of duds.

That worth of Self Accomplishment also gave him permission to have a beer since it was now Happy Hour and alcohol was half price. He found even More Pride in Himself which extended into the evening after being able to successfully stop, "after just Two glasses," drinking that sweet nectar which poured from the Gods liquor taps.

Budweiser.

Mr. Jefferson's mall experience also went better than planned too.

He just happened to run into officer Kunkle while heading towards the changing room.

Pete was More Than Willing to give JJ a Personal Hand and if he needed anything other than that, then he had Kunkle's permission to take it.

And Take It JJ Did.

The Two spent over an hour playing dress up and hide the sausage in more than one business outlets changing room.

Mr. Jefferson lost count after their fourth sexual excursion.

Just as the evening was starting to wrap up as most businesses were getting ready to lock their doors for the night, Pete was hoping, "More Like Begging," to follow JJ back to his pad.

But Jarrett wasn't going for it.

After his last screw up, the only person he was having sex with in his house was Jean.

Kunkle's youthful and heartless response to the man's unreasonable answer caused an outcome that he was never expecting. Detective Jefferson ordered the Department's Newbie to turn around and walk away.

RIGHT!
FUCKING!
NOW!

I know that You and Everyone Else are One Hundred Percent Positive that my wife left me, and I just need to get over it and move on, but Your Shitty Ass Attitude just blew Any and All Chances of me and you ever hooking up again, NOW, GET THE FUCK OUT OF MY SITE!

Because if you do not, I will chalk up your missing report as another one of S.S.K's Victims.

Pete's facial response was enough for JJ to understand that he had gotten through to the boy.

And as Kunkle and the Detective went their separate ways, JJ made one last threat.

I will not only out you at the department and tell the office of investigation about the golden shower you took after taking my last drug test sample. But I'll also spill the beans about your Daddy Dutch if you ever speak about what we are talking about Right Now.

UNDERSTAND BOY.

And being the perfect sub that Pete was expected to be, JJ knew that he could trust his Yes Sir answer.

As Jarrett began to head back home, rabbit hole after rabbit hole did their best to occupy his focus and ability to drive. More than a few times, Mr. Jefferson scraped the curb as he joyfully recollected his night out on the town.

His cock was getting harder and harder as he continued to drive home.

That also was making it almost impossible to concentrate.

But all that smoke and mirrors quickly ended the moment he pulled into his personal driveway. The Always Closed garage door was slightly cracked and its interior light was on. There also appeared to be some sort of shadowed movement taking place within.

Someone was in his house.

Jarrett's first thought was that Mr. Kunkle wasn't going to take no for an answer.

The little shit had probably squeezed himself through that Eight Inch slot and was hopefully trying to get his hungry ass ready before his new I Want You For My Daddy, could make it home.

That idea quickly faded though.

If Pete was inside, then Were The Hell is his sports car.

JJ understood that the Canary Yellow MG Midget could easily be hid, but he would have had to garaged it at a neighbor's house just to hide it.

The streets in Jarrett's part of the subdivision were long, wide, and opened.

And due to the Neighborhood's Covenant Contract, everyone had to sign before buying, homeowners were NOT ALLOWED to leave their cars sitting in the streets after dark. All Vehicles must be either garaged or parked in the driveway.

If it was found blocking traffic after Eleven P.M, the automobile will be towed.

And they meant it Too because Mr. Jefferson still has the towing ticket to prove it.

So, Pete's car would have stuck out like a sore thumb on these empty streets because it wasn't even Ten O'clock yet.

Kind of like that beast sitting between the darkened shadows of two broken streetlights. Something that will be called in tomorrow morning and demanded to be instantaneously fixed.

That power was un unexpected benefit until the day Officer Jarrett called about a pothole out in front of his house. Arapahoe County had a crew out there fixing it before he had a chance to leave for work that day.

And this would be his third time using that Power when it came to getting the neighborhood street lights fixed.

Sneaking around back with his gun drawn, JJ was about to step through the glass sliding doors, when he heard the garage door open. It seems that the culprit was heading for the hills as the homeowner was entering from the back.

Jarrett should have completely followed his training before relaxing though.

Seeing that the house was ransacked, and the lap top Jean had given him was missing from the kitchen counter, the Detective began to let his guard down.

Especially after a quick search of the premises before

making sure the garage door was still open.

It left him a way out, if needed.

It also gave the intruder an escape outlet just in case they were still somewhere inside.

Burglars tend not to get violent if there isn't a feeling of entrapment.

As JJ went to call this in, he should have checked the coat closet that was behind him next to the front door.

If he had, the officer would have noticed the man with a full syringe of morphine in his left hand and he maybe would have also noticed the Ether filled rag in his right. Jarrett could possibly have also realized at that time he and the cinnamon smelling intruder have met before.

More than once already.

While the Grim Reaper tried to wrap his left hand around the phone and over Mr. Jefferson's mouth and nose, Graves right hand tried shoving the needle deep into the right side of JJ's neck, but something was in the way.

What Skinner did not realize was that Arapahoe's Detective was still holding onto his service revolver.

The randomly forced shot that exploded from the gun turned out to be Mr. Jefferson's saving grace, before the Ether's darkness overtook him.

It seems that it doesn't take but a small breath of the stuff, before the body begins to act.

It also seems that it doesn't take more than one bullet to run off an attacker.

Before collapsing and slamming the back of his head onto their tiled floor, JJ could have sworn that the intruder made some sort of comment about needing to quickly grab something before he could leave.

That something was found in the refrigerator a few minutes after the Calvary arrived.

As the Detective was being checked out in the back of an ambulance, Dutch came over carrying an evidence bag with something in it.

It was another skin sample slide.

Except this slide was unlike any other.

Instead of it presenting with just JJ's initials, the sample also held a piece of his skin that had been carved off the homeowner's right shoulder.

And it had the same date as his last one.

Its numeration consisted of just Two Numbers and a slash. Three slash Zero.

It looked as if S.S.K. had left a cinnamon scented gift for his investigator.

Skinner was either giving him Thirty days or until the Years end.

Either way, there was No Doubt that Arapahoe County's Serial Killer was coming for the Department's Lead Detective that was handling the case.

A Mr. Jarrett Sage Jefferson

CH. 12
TAG, YOU'RE IT.

As JJ walked into the department that very next morning, it appeared as if he had become the latest gossip at the company's water cooler. And they would have kept talking if it hadn't been for him speaking up.

Seems JJ's makeover had done the trick.

Do to his lack of smell and unkept appearance, Randel's Best Friend had smoothly blended into the busy background of everything that was now occurring concerning the case involving S.S.K.

You should see where he took my skin sample after knocking me out, was Jarrett's opening statement to being in the room.

And their what the fuck responses brought a smile to the Detective's face.

Something that rarely happens these days.

As the group stood around shooting the shit, JJ's desk phone began to ring.

It was a young girl and by the sound of her voice, Mr. Jefferson could tell that she was Very Afraid.

Mandy Bartlett was running one of Bart's storage units and he had gotten a hold of her earlier that day before he and his wife went missing. He had given orders that if something were to happen to him, she was supposed to Immediately contact Detective Jarrett.

She had tried the day after Mr. and Mrs. Bartholomew went missing, but it was his day off.

The employee was frightened for her life and was hoping for some protection.

To get that, Mandy was holding back some information until JJ gave his word that he would stop by and check on her.

Daily!

She was even hoping that, "Maybe," Arapahoe's investigation team would be willing to post a car at the unit she worked at.

Mr. Jefferson could not promise a car, but JJ did Guarantee that he would swing by before the day was over. The Detective even went so far as to say that he would personally hang around during his off time.

But for her to get that kind of attention, he needed to know what was so important that Bart had an employee reach out to him.

And that's when the case took a step forward.

She found Two phone numbers related to their crime scenes.

Mandy wasn't sure the first one she had it was an actual number.

There was something familiar about it.

As the gal spoke; Jarrett couldn't help but to sing it with Mandy as she spouted out Eight, Six, Seven, Five, Three, Zero, Nine.

JJ's laughing response was not the reaction she was expecting.

In fact, being laughed at, almost cost Mr. Jefferson his witness as she was about to hang up in utter disgust. The Detective's explanation that the number actually went to a song and after singing the numbers back to her, Mandy settled down as the startled worker remembered why they had sounded So Familiar.

JJ was excited to realize that they had struck gold with the other number.

Well, sort of.

After promising Mandy that he would stop by later that afternoon, Officer Jefferson began dialing Seven, Two, Zero dash Eight, Eight, Eight dash Five, Six, One, Two, and ended up waiting for what felt like a life time before a Very Young sounding child picked up and answered the phone.

And like most kids, getting an answer out of the little shit was tougher than pulling a rotten tooth from a stubborn jackass.

The phone number belonged to a pay phone.

Something JJ has only seen in pictures.

He had no idea that some of the antiquities still existed.

It was while trying to get the Talkies location that the young man started to become hostile and belligerent. His Asshole response of I'm Not Google Dickhead was quickly followed up with the phone being slammed back down on the receiver.

Before JJ decided to give the phone company a call so that he could trace the ring-a-dings location, the frazzled officer had to take a moment and calm down.

He was still angry and wishing the kid had been standing here so that he could ring the little Bastard's Got Dam Throat.

Kid's these days were missing the one thing that kept JJ's generation in line.

The end of a parent's belted hand.

Someone needs to bring back corporal punishment when it came to the privacy of a family's personal drama.

It always amazed the Detective how Right-Wing Christians SCREAMED to bring back a bible-based lifestyle, but when it comes to that verse which says (Withhold not correction from the child: for if thou beats him with the rod, he shall Not Die. Thou shalt beat him with the rod, and shalt deliver his soul from Hell,) These fanatics were also the FIRST to SCREAM CHILD ABUSE, CHILD ABUSE.

That is why their beliefs and practices always fall on deaf ears these days.

Especially with Mr. Jefferson.

He Hated Fucking Hypocrites.

As JJ sat at his desk waiting for the phone company to return his call because they were not even sure there was a phone at that location, the rabbit holes of I Wonder began to call out to the Detective.

And So Did Officer Long from across the room.

TIME STARTS NOW!

As Jarrett sat with the evidence inside his head, the thought of just how long S.S.K.'s reign of terror might be, began to sink into the I Hope Not pile.

They know for sure that the killer was working during the Nineteen Eighties.

And now that there were two pillaged units, JJ was having to guess just what kind of missing evidence had been lost.

If their contents were the same, then the dates associated with those missing skin samples would either go backward into the Seventies or they would forwardly continue into the Nineties.

It was the future that JJ was betting on.

Since the Department had been able to secure Skinner's eighties memorabilia, Jarrett was willing to bet the Two storage units that were breached might have contained the Nineteen Nineties and the Two Thousands.

The sure-fire thing now, was could they find and secure The Twenty Tens, the Twenty Twenties, and the year they were currently in.

Twenty Thirty.

With his desk phone ringing and Tom shouting out TIME, JJ's rabbit hole quickly collapsed.

The phone company was returning the Detective's call.

Service agent Dalia, "like Jarrett," was Just as Amazed that there was one still in existence.

It seems that this forgotten about phone's address was listed as Six, Seven, One, Five, South Cornerstone Way.

With it being well into the lunch hour and the phone's location just around the corner, Jefferson decided to have lunch first. Then he would head over to the company it was addressed too and see why such an antique was still in existence.

Seems the business owner was INSISTING that its number would Never be discontinued or disconnected

He was even willing to pay out of pocket for any and all charges pertaining to its repair and upkeep.

It was that realization the phone was attached to a Meat Market and Deli, which changed the Detectives lunch plans.

JJ would just head over there, right here and now.

There was just something about its name that sparked Jarrett's curiosity.

The company went by the name of Graves.

While Mr. Jefferson was gathering his belongings before heading out the door, Androids With Real Skin were blasting their next promotion across the public airways of Colorado's front range.

At AWRS, We Continually Strive For Perfection.

If Your Synthetic sounds More Like a Dog's Squeaky Toy, It's time to give up the Latex and Plastic.

Why Settle For
FAKE SKIN,
When You Can Have
REAL.
Look For A
REAL SKIN DEALER
Near You.

Unlike some people, the commercials for AWRS always gave JJ a little bit of the creeps.

He wasn't sure about having sex with a machine: let alone one that felt as if it had Real Skin.

The widower has always said that the best and easiest way for Artificial Intelligence to imprison us, was to get man to drop their pants. And once it had us erotically enchanted, we would do any and everything The Machine asked or demanded from its sexually enslaved subjects.

His best friend John Randal was proof of that.

That man would sell his soul just to own a personal android.

Especially if it came with Real Skin.

Seems the Synthetic is capable of physically performing every sexual position and act that is downloaded into its personal data banks.

They even had the ability to self-clean themselves now.

John is still bragging about his last encounter.

The company had to increase the bots agility and capabilities after its Kama Sutra encounter with Randal.

He Actually Broke The Damned Thing.

JJ, "to this day," still insist that John get help for his sexual addiction before he ends up physically hurting someone. But since the arrival of AWRS's optional choices for a sturdy and willing partner, Jarrett's concerns do nothing but fall on John's deaf and unwilling to listen to your Bullshit ears.

As Arapahoe's Detective pulled into the parking spot sitting in front of the phone, the business greeted its customers with an exceptionally large and welcoming sign.

The artwork had that Twenties design and feel.

JJ actually Loved its nostalgia.

The Twenty by Forty Ellipsed Circle was painted Bright Red and had a Forest Green Outline.

Inside the Ellipse the name GRAVES was painted in Bright White and took over the entire top half of the inner circle. The words Meat Market and Deli were also in stark white and took half of the lower circles' location.

And below that was the companies phone number.

Nowhere near the one JJ was investigating.

By the look of the structure's outward brick design, it was certainly built around the mid to late Eighties. Most buildings these days are Three-D printed and come without all the extra fuss and mess these dinosaurs demanded.

Their antiquated windows didn't even collect or store solar power for the structure's usage.

But once JJ walked through their double glass doors, All Was Forgiven.

The Intoxicating smell of meat in all its stages and forms quickly overwhelmed Mr. Jefferson. And just like the other hypnotized customers, the Detective stood there swaying to the smell of Fresh cut and cooking bacon.

Every form of sweet breads, sausages, and other meat choices that were needing to be cured before getting sold, hung not just above their showcase counters but above every table out in the dining room also.

If someone wanted to go and spend the rest of their lives in Meat Heaven, Graves was the place to die at.

As their newest and First Time Ever customer began to look around, the hungry rumbling in Jarrett's belly quickly noticed that there was not a vegetable in site. This wonderful Place was ONE HUNDRED PERCENT VEGAN FREE.

That revelation instantly sent the Officer into Overdrive as he began to look for the chair that would eventually become his grave marking headstone.

Meat.

MEAT.

MEAT!

And That's When JJ saw it.

As the front counter off to his right made a ninety-degree turn, a Fully-Fledged Butcher Shop was in full swing.

Their Fresh Ground Fifty Cents a Pound hamburger was FLYING out the door.

Because of the Special Way Mr. Graves handled and seasoned the meat, employees couldn't keep it stocked fast enough.

They were usually sold out before the dinner rush began.

According to the little red head who was answering JJ's questions, that was their number one selling product.

That is, except for today.

Graves's Meat Pies always sold out hours before the Sabbath started later in the evening.

He had no doubt that they did, after a woman referred to as Hi June, stopped in to pick up her order of Fifty before being reminded to tell her sister Beth that Amy said Hi.

And after purchasing Two pounds of the grounded version to pick up and take with him after having a chance to sit down and eat himself, Jarrett found out later that evening its unusual flavor was Quite Addicting.

He also discovered from the little talker that Mr. Graves had taken the week off from working inside the store because he just recently lost his parents.

Seems they were taken at the same time.

That freebie was the reason the Detective considered this Graves being unrelated to John and Ruth Graves.

His Graves went missing Six Months and Fifty Years ago.

His last question to the Canadian sounding counter clerk about the phone outside was one he was not expecting but should have considered.

Mr. Graves likes authenticity when it comes to nostalgia.

Gotta keep up the image, Ya know.

After Making Sure to grab a brochure, "and adding a mental note to Purposely Come Back," Mr. Jefferson took his time to tour every last crook and cranny of this Marvelous Theme Park of Meats.

If Jean were still around, this restaurant would have been placed on his bucket list of things to do after she dies and is No Longer in control of JJ's eating choices. There was no way IN HELL his wife would ever have let her sexy and One Percent body fat Hunk anywhere near a place such as this.

His wash board stomach rubbing between her legs as she saddle rode his sturdy and Rock-Hard hips was an orgasm inducer that she was UNWILLING to give up.

CH. 13
NOT AGAIN.

The widowed officer was just about to settle into that image of Jean sexually bouncing on his lap in the Charger's front seat when Becky's voice came crackling over the radio.

JJ, Skinner has struck again.

This time it was another storage unit in the same vicinity as their first crime scene.

And JJ, the girl you talked with earlier, "Mandy Bartlett," is the one missing.

It was that announcement which almost caused the officer to bite down on the tip of his own service revolver.

Why The Hell Hadn't a Patrolman Been Sent Over there to Protect her.

Budget cuts.

That's Why!

The Department had no way of sparing a dozen or so officers to look after those who were still managing Bart's storage units.

There Were Just To Many Of Them.

And if that Had Been A Possibility, the time it would have taken to coordinate the Investigative Departments of TEN COUNTIES concerning only Bartholomew's units was beyond comprehension.

There would also have been the interest of searching every other business that was like his too.

By the time that miracle of just where to start occurred, Skinner could be in the wind and long gone.

So, "for now," Dutch was ordering his department to keep the investigation quiet and contained to just Arapahoe County. And if their fact-finding mission just so happened to cross over into another District, they would deal with that issue later.

Something Every Detective in the Chief's unit Quickly and UNANIMOUSLY agreed upon.

As JJ sat in his car gathering his wits before heading out in Mandy's direction, his tearful thoughts couldn't help but wish for better days. The United States, "just like every other country out there," was still recovering from an Economic Disaster that Started Ten Years Ago.

An Extreme Virus decided to take a trip around the globe.

It took a Full Five Years to gain control of the outbreak.

By the time it was over with, millions were dead.

Third World Countries had it the hardest.

Their death tolls extended into the Tens of Millions.

If it wasn't for home-based business's such as Graves, many towns in the united states would have vanished. Revived trades such as candle making, butchers, cobblers, seamstress's, and midwives quickly filled the void of our DEMOLISHED OPTIONS THAT LIFE SUCKING CORPORATIONS PROVIDED.

Doctors, nurses, and teachers associated with medicine were some of the Highest Casualties when the Plague first hit.

That list of the dead quickly extended to those who were associated with them.

Then so on.

And So On.

Before the United States lost a years' worth of contact with the outside world, it was reported that North Korea was killing anyone who sneezed and sniffled. The Catholic Church's Pope also had the snots and sniffles the last time he was seen.

Mr. Jefferson never heard anything about the Deity after that last broadcast concerning the older man's well-being.

To This Day, JJ was not sure how He and Jean survived those first Five Years.

With him being in law enforcement, He and his fellow

workers had been placed on the front lines of defense and order.

It still blows Jarrett's mind that first day martial law had been declared.

Something that was never expected to happen in The United States.

But once our countries armed forces took over Every Major City; the revelation that this shit storm was not some bad movie being played out amongst the public, shocked every last civilian to our core.

And now here the Detective was being shocked once more.

His current witness was missing.

The look on the Precinct Chief's face said all that was needing to be said once Jarrett arrived at the scene.

Their Department had missed the Mark.

Not only was the cinnamon scented office ransacked like the others, but all evidence out in the vacated storage unit, "INCLUDING MANDY," was gone and now missing too.

Mandy Bartlett was Declared one of S.S.K's Victims on Zero slash Seven slash Zero slash Eight slash Three slash Zero.

It was at this point that JJ wasn't quite sure what to do next.

She had mentioned the possibility of others; but in his haste, Mr. Jefferson forgot to ask about them and was also just planning on getting those answers once he got here.

But, it seems Skinner had beaten him to the scene once again.

The icing on that cake was provided by the Serial Killer after the crime techs opened the studio apartments refrigerator.

There were TWO skin sample slides.

One was presumably Mandy's and the other belonged to JJ

The only reason that second sample was a positive on the scene match was due to S.S.K. leaving JJ's initials and the same date as the last slide that was identified as his.

JJ, Three slash Zero.

Jarrett had chalked up his One Inch skin gouge to Skinner being in a hurry, for he seemed to purposely take more than what was needed for a slide.

And now, the Detective knew why.

The cat wanted his mouse to know that he was coming for him and was willing to take his own sweet time.

But the sly smile that spread across JJ's lips showed a more mischievous response.

This dude must have never seen an episode of Tom and Jerry. If he had, S.S.K. would know that he needed to be looking over his shoulder and watching his own back. Because this Jerry, "Like Tom's Jerry," was Now out for blood.

Jean's widowed husband was so ready to call it a day.

His emotions had been left Bloodied and Raw After unsuccessfully promising the gal that she was safe, and nothing would happen to her.

So on the edge of Extreme were JJ's feelings, that he couldn't force himself to buck up and just go home.

Something he was Not Willing to do.

Jarrett was afraid of being alone and haunted by Two Women who might be seeking vengeance for his lack of follow through.

Back at the Department, there was a rarely used room that had been transformed into sleeping quarters during the plague. The Thirty by Thirty-foot section had a fully functioning restroom with private changing quarters and Twenty Bunkbeds.

Other than some fresh out of the academy cadet pulling the night oil in hopes of an early promotion, Jarrett was fairly sure he would have the place all to himself.

It seems that his unexpected presence had interrupted someone's Ten O'clock rendezvous.

Whoever it was, had scampered out the back rooms exit just as he was unlocking the darkened quarters front entrance door.

In their hurried exit, the pair of swinging unused handcuffs gave away their last location and possible intent of tonight's kinky exhibition that was unknowingly going to take place in this unmanned section of iniquity.

That was a blessing to JJ.

He was in no listening mood to someone else's bump and grind transgressions.

If and when he gets to feeling better, maybe they can reschedule for another night. He Loves to watch and was a little bit of an exhibitionist himself.

Jean Loved it when she got to experience the handcuffs.

The little Dominatrix Really Got off on the nights JJ gave up the keys and surrendered to his Vixens every wish and demand.

He never really understood Just How Kinky a woman could be until he surrendered the reigns that first time when he was somewhere around Twenty-One or Maybe Twenty-Two. By the time Jean was through fulfilling her fantasies, the young husband had become an Instantaneous Addict.

One Hit from her Extreme and Dominating Lovemaking was all it took.

As the Departments Exhausted officer slid down the sexual rabbit hole of memories, JJ's hand sank down the front of his briefs.

Jean might not be with him at this physical moment, but his hand and her memories were.

While her widowed husband was lost in his lustful thoughts, the You Have a Message light on his desk phone started blinking only a few moments after he left out of the office earlier that morning.

It was a message from Mandy Bartlett.

Miss Bartlett found another storage unit under that first number she had given him and this one had a second and officially working phone number listed with the rental. There is also a man currently outback emptying the unit that we have associated with here at My Premises.

He's already removed some kind of barber's chair and is currently packing up what may be light boxes or some sort of back lit shadow box.

I'm Really scared Detective.

I wish that I were able to tell you what kind of vehicle he is using, but I have never seen anything of that nature.

It's not a truck, van nor is it a suburban.

The thing is Really Old though.

There is also a chance that the vehicle is Red in color, but it's hard to make out do to how dirty it is.

As she continued to whisper into the phone, Mandy was also trying to describe the man, but the way he is dressed was making an actual identification impossible. What she could say was that he is bald, possibly white and elderly.

By his height, he may be somewhere around six foot, but her viewing distance and trying not to be spotted was making it hard.

Listening to the Manager's scared whimpering that following day was making JJ's morning start that much more difficult. Especially with the entire department standing around the Detective's desk, as they all took part in the debriefing surrounding his case and its newest missing person.

By the way Mandy's tears were starting to overwhelm her, they knew she was in trouble.

Skinner has never left a living witness at the scene of his crimes.

Well, except for Detective Jarrett.

But that interaction between the Two was Nothing More than fun and games to S.S.K.

If this call had been intercepted yesterday, Mandy would More Than Likely still be alive.

But, it wasn't.

Everyone in the Investigation room already knew the outcome of this phone call.

Sadly, they would All get to listen, "First Hand," to just how it ended.

As Mandy quickly realized that she still had some information that was vital to the Department's case, the scared girl said a whimpered prayer as she left the window and headed over to the office computer.

She found another number associated with the units.

That second number was Seven, Two, Zero, Eight, Eight, Eight, followed by Five and that is when the shit hit the fan.

The gal was never able to calmly say those last three digits.

Just as she was about to say something that sounded like Hicks, Vicks or Six, they heard the Facilities front door get kicked in.

Mandy was never able to clearly sound out the last Two Numbers either, as she began to fight for her life.

Some said she yelled twelve, while others were certain that they were nothing more than gurgled curse words as she was being either killed or subdued. There were even speculations that someone was making comments about going to the Grave.

Whatever was said, was said quickly.

It sounded like the room began to explode after that.

The perpetrator was destroying anything and everything he could get his hands on.

And this entire time, not one peep came from the extremely freckled red headed Irish woman.

Her attacker did give out a pretty heavy grunt though, as it sounded like he was picking up something heavy. Those who were still listening, all agreed that he was probably carrying out Mandy's body at that time.

Many of JJ's colleagues were also doing their best to assure him that he had not made a mistake by tracking down that pay phone before heading out to see her.

There was no way of knowing who, what, when or where Skinner was planning to attack next. He did all that was asked from him and no one here in the Department felt as if he had let them or Mandy down.

This just happened to be one of those days were snake eyes where the only outcome.

Kind of like what was currently happening to Skinner's latest victim.

The dice roll had Not been in her favor either.

Nor would be her next game of chance after that.

S.S.K. was going to make sure of it.

CH. 14
ONE DOWN AND ONE TO GO.

As her head still swirled within the Ether induced sedation, the commotion surrounding Mandy started stirring those last memories of what took place back at the office of Mile-High storage.

Because there was no knock or any kind of heads up, the young woman did not have enough time to find something for self-defense just in case the situation called for it. The man that had been outback cleaning up his rental, came busting in through the studio apartments front door as she was leaving Detective JJ a message.

The linebacker sized attacker had Mandy in his sights the second that door shattered from him bashing it in.

The Very small framed gal stood no chance.

The business manager was just hoping that her last SCREAMS containing the final digits to the related phone number had been audible enough for them to understand. Her attacker was forcing a soaked rag over Mandy's face as she was trying to shout out this important clue.

The clue that just might end up saving her life.

Mile high's office manager also called out the one thing that would have cracked the Case surrounding Skinner's verification. But that shot of morphine being shoved into her neck at the same time, caused his identity to come out as nothing more than a garbled mess of tongue twisting verbiage.

Even though she shouted out Graves; Arapahoe's Investigative Department couldn't understand her muffled voice.

While those last memories swirled their Horrifying remembrance in the drug induced victim, Mandy's impaired vision was starting to detect another shuffle taking place in her vicinity. Someone smelling as if they had bathed in cinnamon was forcefully removing something from her subdued location.

As her frightened senses quickly seemed to instantaneously return, S.S.K. was dragging a bound and unknown occupant from their caged environment.

The dark-skinned woman was trying to fight back, but the way she and Mandy were chained would not allow such heroic efforts. Both women were wearing a metal collar that was padlocked from behind the neck.

They also had about a Three-Foot piece of chain that ran from the rear part of the neck jewelry down to their doubly shackled ankles.

Mandy's Hands were also bent up and cuffed behind her at the chains midway point.

Just like the woman who was currently being taken from their cage as she Heroically tried to fight for her life.

A battle that would be unsuccessful; a result skinner's current victim was quickly going to find out.

That is when Mandy also realized that she would be losing this bout to live also.

As S.S.K's caged victim fought her way up into a kneed position, the nude victim suddenly figured out that there was no gag in place that would keep her from SCREAMING For Help.

A questionable answer to which she soon found out why.

Not only was her imprisoned location all the way out in bum fucked nowhere, but her captor had an addiction to an Extremely Horrible Pleasure.

He LOVES to hear the SCREAMS of his captives.

Their final dying chokes were like music to his ears.

Every Skin Tingling Echo.

While Mandy kneeled in complete disbelief, her captor hooked up another chain belonging to an electric lift attached to the ceiling and began to raise his next project.

Once he had her lifted and swung over the cutting board, Skinner walked over to a side table to which he returned to the cussing woman with a fresh syringe in his right hand. As her threats fell on the captor's deaf ears, the balding man leaned in and spoke the words that would end up leaving a lasting impression on Mandy as she waited her turn on the table of death.

Because I want to keep you alive until the very end, I'm going to give you just enough to dull only the pain.

I Will not make the same mistake I made on your little Oriental girlfriend.

It seems that he had miscalculated Ti's weight and ended up overdosing the Very Small Framed Asian Woman.

He was Absolutely pissed at himself after Aniqua began SCREAMING that she was allergic to morphine. Something the caged woman quickly realized was an absolute blessing as she watched her soul mate get skinned from head to foot by the creepy man with a set smile on his, "This Is Quite Enjoyable," face.

The SCREAM that erupted from Aniqua's soul once that hidden view of what was around the corner came into sight, sent Mandy cowering in her caged prison.

HE'S EATING US!

HE'S EATING US, were her last audible words before the drug began to kick in.

With her limp body finally settling down in her hanging chained prison, Skinner began to lower Aniqua's body onto his butchery table. And with her lack of resistance, it only took a few moments for him to strap this week's special onto the slab.

That is when Mandy just happened to notice, "just like S.S.K's current victim," she had also been shaved from head to foot.

Even her makeup and nail polish had been removed.

Just like an animal awaiting its turn at the slaughterhouse, Skinner already had her prepped and ready for processing.

The SCREAMS that poured from within Miss. Bartlett's

encaged environment would end up being the first OF MANY that day.

Her second set of SCREAMS soon followed, when Mandy watched her captor take a scalpel and began to run its Razor Sharpened Edge down the backside of the subdued woman who was going into his next batch of charcuterie.

Aniqua's thick hips and upper leg portions were going to make the perfect meat to dry cure before selling it as Prosciutto.

The amount of Rillettes, Pate and Mousse from her liver and fatty meat portions should fill his store shelves for At Least a month.

The Salami and Chorizo sections were starting to get low, so that was on the list to fill also.

What was left, would go into this week's hamburger deliveries to Denver's homeless shelters.

Something that he has been happy to do for the last Twenty Years.

As Mandy tried her best Not to watch what was going on at the table that was maybe Five or so feet from her, the prisoner just couldn't keep herself from taking a peak now and then as the LIVE Horror Movie was occurring .

Her captor was taking his sweet ass time as The Killer was Pleasurably Enjoying how it felt peeling the skin from his bound AND STILL ALIVE victim.

The fixed smile on his face said it all.

S.S.K. WAS LOVING EVERY EXCRUTIATING MINUTE OF IT!

Even though Aniqua was fully aware of what was happening to her, the morphine was keeping her in a helpless and subdued state.

It also seemed that the butcher was an expert in his craft.

After slicing her from the forehead all the way down to the lower back; Two proceeding slices from that point continued down each leg, around the heel and across the bottoms of her feet.

Another cut went from the back hand of Aniqua's left index

finger, up the arm, across the back, to where it proceeded down and along her other arm. Skinner's scalpel didn't stop until it reached that opposite index finger on his victim's right hand.

His next move was that unwanted scene in a movie to which No One could divert their eyes.

He began to Hand Peel the skin apart from his STILL ALIVE Captive.

That next set of drug induced SCREAMS did not erupt from Miss. Brown until the subdued woman saw a peeled part of the skull cap in her peripheral vision.

Once those SCREAMS of revelation began to reverberate within the small confined space of the warehouse where Mr. Graves practiced his butchery craft, Mandy's Overly shocked senses had no choice but to join in with Aniqua's.

As the hope for rescue began to fade within the two women, their COMBINED SCREAMS seemed to rock Skinner's spirit like a Perfectly Orchestrated Duet.

The man looked as if he actually orgasmed while standing at Aniqua's side.

It was the look of contentment that made Mandy realize that this day would be her last.

Unless someone Miraculously busted through the steel enforced door, there would be no living through what was about to occur to her.

It seems that the only way she was leaving this location would be in his daily meat grinding special. The next thought that popped into the bound woman's head caused an unexpected and muffled giggle to erupt from within.

Her brother Mickey had fallen onto hard times after refusing to get help for his meth addiction.

He was currently staying at a shelter.

If her brother had any inkling that he might be eating his sister in the next day or so, she was willing to bet that Quinten would finally go straight and get some help after that.

Who wouldn't?

Especially, if they somehow found out that the man she

recognized as Mr. Graves was selling human meat to the homeless and those Arrogant Yuppies who shopped at his Meat Market.

It wasn't until Skinner's Favorite commercial began to play on the radio that was set in the background on low, did he finally slow down and take a break.

AWRS was promoting their latest commercial.

And it was an ironic one at that.

We here at Androids With **REAL SKIN**, We Love to hear our Lovers Scream.

But that sexual response only happens when Skin touches Skin.

Latex Synthetics cannot do that, But Ours Can.

Why Settle For

FAKE SKIN,

When You Can Have

REAL.

Look For A

REAL SKIN DEALER

Near You.

Her captor seemed to be OVERLY Excited and kept mumbling something under his breath that Mandy wasn't able to make out quite so well.

The intangible words sounded like; they are going to Love this next batch of skins.

But she could not be sure if that response were related to the commercial or those he was planning on feeding.

Either thought was just Too Mind Shattering to consider.

Just like what was now about to take place at the butchery block of iniquity.

Skinner was sliding over another table that was attached to the ceiling.

As the platform was leveled out, he lowered the plexiglass board down onto the exposed muscle of his victim whose skin was now removed from the entire back portion of her body.

Turning Miss. Brown into an actual sample slide, the butcher locked the plates together before raising them up and spinning Aniqua One Hundred and Eighty Degrees. Once that was achieved, she was secured to the new table before her now faced up body reappeared from underneath the one that was being removed.

As that first butcher's table was slid away, Mandy could have sworn Aniqua gave her a side glance of hopelessness.

The tears running down her face professed what was in her heart.

She was saying goodbye to the only person who would witness her death.

The crying woman was also shedding a few tears because her and Ti had eaten at his Market on more than one occasion.

And now some unsuspecting soul was going to eat her.

More than likely, Her Auntie!

That woman loved Mr. Graves's sweetbreads and Liver Pate.

She served it every Wednesday night when the women from her church gathered for their weekly bible study that always ended up turning into a drunken game of bridge and gossip.

As Mandy cowered in her kneeled position of subdued servitude; the captive did everything she could to divert her Shocked eyes as S.S.K. began to deglove the rest of his current project, after he administered that next round of numbing morphine.

Starting at Aniqua's feet, Skinner made sure to focus so that he would not damage the merchandise while peeling the skin from her toes.

Tears and rips lower the pricing value.

Something that he was unwilling to accept.

That is where the perfectionist who lives inside of him comes in handy.

Mandy got to see and hear it in person, as he slowly took his time in those specific areas where accidents can happen.

The toes, fingers, sex organs and women with large breast.

Their perfect removal took the one word he kept repeating to himself over and over and over.

Patience Mr. Graves.

Patience.

Patience.

Patience.

As the last of Aniqua's Heavenly symposium with her captor began to play the final cords to her muffled and dying SCREAMS, Mandy unfortunately just happened to glance up as Skinner was Firmly grasping the last portions of skin that was still attached to the colored woman's face.

Miss. Bartlett looked on in Shocked Horror, as the Realization that the woman strapped to the table was STILL ALIVE and getting a First Hand View of HER OWN FACE being peeled off.

That next SCREAM to erupt from Both Women was while Aniqua's Lidless eyes looked over at Mandy after the last of her identity was removed in one Quick Yank.

While his caged victim had an Uncontrolled SCREAMING Fit, Skinner's smiling graze locked eyes with Mandy as he began to roll up the now dead woman's skin. S.S.K. popped an Extremely Obvious wood as he stood there drowning in the Operetta of Mandy's current release.

Just to make sure that she would end up giving her Ultimate performance, Mr. Graves decided that she would be needing a change of scenery for that Grand reception.

That's when he pulled out his cock and wiggled it at the gal before she passed out.

And after dragging Miss. Bartlett's collapsed body over to the table and giving his next victim a place of Honor, Mandy finally got to see what her captor was hiding just around the corner.

Skinner's personal and private man cave.

A One-Man butchery and curing shop.

CH. 15
HELLO CLAIRICE, I MEAN MANDY.

Seeing firsthand just what happened with Aniqua, Mandy knew that it would not do her any good fighting back when Skinner came to get her.

Something he seemed to be quite disappointed about.

She didn't even scream when the mechanical lift felt like it was trying to pull her arms out of their shoulder sockets.

But that perseverance didn't last long; because Mandy Did SCREAM when she saw what was about to happen to the gal who had been deskinned just a few minutes ago. Just as S.S.K. lifted her head so that he could make sure the injection in Mandy's neck took, the body less heads of Aniqua, her partner Ti and a few others were staring back at Skinner's next slab of beef.

As the warm drug induced elixir began to spread through Miss. Bartlett's veins, all thoughts of how to get herself out of this mess began to spread themselves thin upon Mandy's list of things to ask.

She was hoping to buy some time so that she could change the man's mind.

The offering of herself as his personal concubine was not out of the realm of possibilities.

The woman was willing to do whatever it took to get out of this life and death situation.

As she tried to concentrate on which question to grasp within the swirling mass of morphine induced illusions that were trying to overwhelm Skinner's play toy, a mumbled wondering of, "what would your parents say," slipped from her numbed lips and tongue.

S.S.K. seemed to find that question laughable.

When she asked it again, his Violent Response was SCREAMED into Mandy's face while he was in the prosses of buckling her wrist to the table.

My Parents Do not, Never Have and Never Will Give A Shit About Me.

And before Mandy could ask why, Skinner offered her the chance to ask them herself.

Unless they were here and still alive, "because the man himself looked as if he was at least in his early to mid-Seventies," the groggy woman had no clue how that impossible miracle was going to happen.

And then Skinner showed her.

John and Ruth Graves have been in this room this entire time.

She just couldn't see them.

In the far back of the darkened room hung racks and racks of dried and curing meets.

Mr. Graves had Twenty-Three distinct types of meat hanging not just from a few sets of movable racks, but there were hundreds of more choices hanging from the ceiling.

Some of the varieties included Prosciutto, Salami, Chorizo, Pepperoni and Pancetta.

On just one rack there were shelves of what appeared to be Bacon and Lard.

As Mary continued to focus on who or what was down that section of the warehouse, tubes of Capocollo, Saucisson, Jamón ibérico and Jamón Serrano stared back at her.

There was even Bologna, Guanciale, Kunchiang and Soppressata hanging from the rafters.

As the countdown continued, she began to recognize many of these choices from the Christmas party Mr. and Mrs.

Bartholomew threw last year.

There was Andouille, Kielbasa, Isaan Sausage, Mortadella and what looked to be Corned Beef.

While skinner was asking if she would like to meet his parents, he also informed Mandy that she would be going into Tomorrow's Special.

Blood Sausage.

Miss. Bartlett was now doing everything within her power not to Scream, but that perseverance Instantly Dissipated once Mr. Graves moved the racks out of Mandy's line of sight.

There appeared to be two people standing against the Semi-darkened rooms far wall.

Those sequestered SCREAMS quickly came once the Six-Foot-Tall light boxes were turned on.

Inside the shadow box like structures were the Head to Toe Skins of Mr. and Mrs. Graves.

The couple were Skinner's Very First Victims.

Back in the day, "when they had decided it was time for them to retire," Bill's Selfish Parents declared that they were moving to Florida.

His Mother and Her arthritis were begging for a warmer climate.

His father's addictive Golfing habit happily agreed to her request.

The thing is their plans Never Considered Him.

They were going to sell everything, "which included the house and Their Entire Business," before taking All The Money and leaving him with NOTHING to start his own life over with. And even though their son has been working in the Barber shop ever since the day Bill first learned how to sweep and mop, none of that mattered once his parents finally decided to retire.

Their Heartless reaction of Fuck You and thanks for your Unconditional and Devoted Service sent Bill over the edge.

He just snapped; was the only response Mr. Graves could give Mandy as she groggily tried to sidetrack Arapahoe's Serial Killer S.S.K. with question after daunting question.

The following one almost got her throat instantaneously cut.

Something she was intentionally hoping for if this situation kept heading for the possible outcome as all his other Special Of The Day victims.

Her Slow and Tormenting death.

Did You Eat Them Too?

The next inquisitive question seemed to not only calm Mr. Graves down, but it also made him well up with pride.

After you killed them, what did you do with all the money.

His outspread arms as he turned, before taking a bow, was accompanied by what you see here Clarise is the bounty from their sacrifice and all that I have worked for.

Graves Meat Market and Deli.

Home of Rare Meats and Unusual Delicacies that used to only be found from around the globe.

That continual supply of the hard to find and get, is the reason he and his business have been on the road to success ever since the day Mr. Graves first opened his doors. And do to his Affordable and Delicious hamburger recipe, people were even willing to get out and buy it from him during those five years a Corona Virus plague tried to take everyone out.

That was also when he realized that it made Perfect Business Sense to start a delivery service.

That unexpected bonus made hunting for meat substitutes so much easier after that.

He now had a reason to not only be out and about during the, "SUPPOSED," World's End; but do to the public demand for his service, the sightings of Graves Red Nineteen Fifty-Three Panel Truck became a commonplace discussion at most dinner tables.

Almost every meal started with; I saw Graves Today, which was usually followed by did you see him too.

Mandy actually thought her nightmare might be over when she seemed to pass out as the drug overwhelmed her petite body. But, no sooner did the darkness overtake her, Mr. Graves VIOLENT Slap Instantaneously brought this latest victim back to reality.

Miss. Bartlett's gargled begging for life pleas, seemed to bring a smile to the man as he raised the woman's head to where her chin could be propped up on the table.

There was something he wanted her to see.

Skinner was making head cheese and was hoping to get a shocked reaction out of his next batch once he removed the boiled heads from this current pot.

And the thing He Loved The Most happened once more. Mandy began to SCREAM.

Especially, when he walked a Skulls falling from the bone flesh over to his current victim so that she could have an up-close view of where her brain bag was headed.

He was almost out of this delicacy and his faithful customer's had reminded Mr. Graves that he needed more.

It wasn't until S.S.K. walked over with the scalpel that Mandy began to finally accept the fact that her time was short. Thankfully, the bound woman's next question ended up getting a Serious rise out of her captor.

You do realize that Detective Jarret will eventually capture you.

His laughable response came as no surprise though.

She has Binged on more than one of the detective shows that seem to be on every channel these days.

The man that was about to kill her and feed what was left of the woman's ground remains to the public, had no fear of Mr. Jarrett Jefferson. In Fact, he was looking forward to catching the mouse that thinks its brave enough to come after him.

The things he had planned for the Officer who took his first collection, were going to take a long time to achieve once he started to skin the Detective.

A Long.

Long.

Time.

Skinner was planning to make every last minute of JJ's Life an Excruciating one.

There would be No sedation for him.

NONE!

WHAT!

SO!

EVER!

Until he attacked the officer at his own home, JJ, "up to then," had No Clue that he was being stalked by S.S.K.

And neither did his next project.

Every last person that was managing a Mile-High storage facility had been warned that their lives might be in danger.

Especially, if they just happened to have one of Skinner's units.

Jarrett tried his best to talk with each manager personally, but there were a few phone calls that went straight to their messaging machine.

As Mr. Graves stood there answering Mandy's nonstop questions, the frightened girl felt the attacker steady her head with his left hand as his scalpel began to make its first of many cuts.

That realization also caused her to produce the first of many Non-Stop SCREAMS.

And it was Heaven to Skinner's ears.

Once he reached the back of her skulls base, S.S.K. tilted the single woman's head forward and gave Miss. Bartlett one of the last views she would ever be receiving this death day.

Thankfully, the morphine had deadened about Ninety Percent of the pain.

Horrifyingly though, the Ten Percent that was lacking, allowed the woman to feel her skin come loose as the Butcher began to lovingly separate it from the muscles tissue.

Skinner, "to help aid in breaking his victims mentally," even went so far as to turn on one of his favorite songs while he worked.

I've Got You Under My skin, By Frank Sinatra.

Once all the cuts that went from head to foot had been made, Mandy Bartlett felt something that no one should EVER experience in their lives.

Skinner's rough and muscular hands as they slid between the skin and underlying tissue.

Instead of using a separating knife for this delicate part, he Preferred the On Hands Method.

As she laid there on his carving table in a semi state of consciousness, the woman who was soon to be dead could feel him gently massage her shoulders as the skin began to separate.

Mandy could also tell that he was teasingly massaging the top of her head, as the skin was pulled from her scalp.

The extra attention given to her gluteus muscles as Mr. Graves took his sexually molesting sweet time to enjoy their perkiness, caused waves of SCREAMING to explode from the dying depths of his current slab of beef.

It wasn't the fact that he seemed to linger in that area which caused Mandy to SCREAM; that reaction was due to the hardening pleasure he was taking in it while rubbing his exposed and stiffening manhood in her bloodied and freshly pealed leg.

Once that second table was slid over and Miss. Bartlett received her bodily mammogram before getting flipped, Mandy knew her time was almost over with.

But, Skinner was doing something to her he had not done with Aniqua.

He was attaching clamps along the entire length of the skins now exposed edges.

As her body began to lift from the cutting board by the same hydraulic wench that had placed her on the table in the first place, the shock of what was happening now began to overwhelm her drug induced sedation.

Especially, when the last of her skin began to rip from its bodily confinement.

While her flesh was raised to the ceiling; the table beneath Mandy was removed, exposing the water tank of spiced and salted brine below.

Having a gut feeling that this would be her last moment on the face of God's Green Earth, Miss. Bartlett took one long and lasting breath before shutting her eyes. What was about to happen next was nothing she wanted to see nor remember.

But as in all Great Horror Movies, her last dying wish was not granted.

As the chains instantaneously dropped her like a death-defying carnival ride, Mandy felt her body rip from the last vestiges of her skin when the lift slammed to a stop just above the tank.

With a light splashing, her deskinned body began to sink within its Three-foot depth.

As the darkness began to envelope her Now Lidless Eyes, Tomorrow's Special got to see her killer turn on the meat grinder for the Blood Sausage that was going to be filled with her remains.

Mandy Bartlett Might have been kidnapped on Zero slash Seven slash Zero slash Eight slash Three slash Zero, but she didn't physically die until Zero slash Seven slash Zero slash Nine slash Three slash Zero.

The department wouldn't realize that information until the day their crime scene technicians had a chance to look over Skinner's man cave.

While Mr. Graves was busy processing the orders for his Marketplace and Deli, His Favorite Company began to announce their latest commercial across the airwaves which served the radio listening public who lived along the Front Range of Colorado's Rocky Mountains.

For Almost Thirty Years, Skinner has been one of AWRS's Main Clients.

And even though his name will Never be found on their record books as either an employee or supplier, those in receiving knew the man on a first name basis.

Mr. Bill Graves.

Someone whose path you Would not want to cross down a darkened and lonely alley way.

He always gave everyone at Androids With REAL SKIN the creeps.

Just dealing with him; always required a game of Rock, Paper or Scissors before the unlucky person who lost had to spend some personal time alone with the man. You could always tell who the looser was, as they tried to fill out the proper paperwork that was required for his deliveries, "In Record Breaking Time."

At AWRS, All Our Synthetics Now Come With REAL SKIN

And when they sweat, You can Actually Taste Their Essence.

Why Settle For
FAKE SKIN,
When You Can Have
REAL.
Look For A
REAL SKIN DEALER
Near You.

CH. 16
GAME TIME.

As JJ walked to his desk inside the Department's Main investigation room; the realization that Mandy Bartlett has now been missing over Twenty-Four Hours, began to sink in.

He had made the frightened woman a promise that there was no possible chance of something happening to her. But Jarrett quickly realized after she went missing that he Never should have made such an impossible deal.

Looking at the list of numbers associated with Bart Bartholomew's business dealings, Mr. Jefferson began making the calls that were needed to warn everyone that still works for the missing man and his wife.

It's been Six Days since they were declared possible victims of S.S.K.

Like Miss. Bartlett, JJ was hoping against all odds that they were somehow still alive.

And the only reason he was willing to chance that belief was due to the lack of bodies.

So Far; every missing person that can Positively be linked back to Skinner, have Never been found alive.

NOT.
ONE.
WHAT.
SO.
EVER.

And even though they are ALL on a Nation-Wide list of the missing, No Remains or any DNA matches have been amongst the located dead.

It was as if his victims seemed to somehow vanish off the face of this earth.

Many in the department have speculated, but no one has hit the nail on the head so far on anyone's whereabouts.

As JJ began to contemplate what may have occurred to them himself, Becky from dispatch just happened to be walking by and was able to sound out the starting gun.

TIME STARTS NOW!

Jarrett knew that Most Serial Killers dispose of the bodies of their victims in out of the way locations. Hell, there are even those that like to dump a Vic's remains out in plain sight.

So far, S.S.K. hasn't been one of those.

At least not yet, anyway.

There's still a chance that they may actually find his Massively Undiscovered Graveyard.

JJ was even considering that the missing may have been sold or used in the sex trade.

Older people like the Bartholomew's had almost limited that possibility until Jarrett remembered that snuff films were a thing too.

The one idea that kept pressing at his what if possibilities, was the consideration that Skinner was a cannibal. But the amount of meat that man would have had to consume was unthinkable.

If S.S.K. had gone that route, He would have eaten himself to death long ago.

Another idea the Detective was considering implausible.

If it were not for that specific commercial Jarrett truly deplored, there was no telling just how long he would have spent down the rabbit hole that day.

It was Randal's Shout out of TIME that finished snapping JJ back into reality.

It seems that this round goes to The Chief, was John's next words.

Mr. Jefferson was just about to ask What The Hell Are You Guys Doing, when his phone began to ring.

It was one of Bart's employees.

The gentleman was responding to the message left on his answering machine.

He's been reaching out to the other managers and so far, no one has a storage unit that is associated with the number that was given to him.

That other number which was lacking a few digits, came back to at least Fifty Units.

The facilities that had something similar to it, would go out and personally check those storage areas. If anything was found, the young man gave his word that the other managers were directed to call the Detective That Very Second.

After making sure to reiterate the fact that they were not to touch anything, JJ decided to head back to Graves Meat Market and Deli.

Not only was it just past lunch, but he was hoping to run into Mr. Graves this time.

He wanted an answer as to why the owner was willing to pay for such Antiquated Tech, when he could just leave a fake one outside for that, "Supposedly," Nostalgic Factor. There was also another thing about his business that was causing the Detective's Deja Vu spot to itch.

The name Graves.

Jarrett was Absolutely Certain that sometime in the past he has had a run in with that name.

The Detective just couldn't seem to put his finger on it yet.

Taking his Twenty, Twelve Dodge Charger over to the Deli, JJ was disappointed once more to find out that he had just missed the man.

If Arapahoe's Finest had been here at Six this morning, Jefferson could have talked with Mr. Graves.

More than likely now, he was out doing his home deliveries and they had No Way of knowing just were those were.

When it came to the Butcher's Personal Customers, that list was kept Private and To Himself.

Just in case he ever got sick, Graves gave it out once to an employee he was willing to trust.

The same employee who unsuccessfully tried pulling the wool over Mr. Graves eyes.

That Son Of A Bitch threatened to take half of the owner's clients when the Bastard said he was going to start His Own marketplace and deli with the owner's personal recipes.

One day while he was cleaning, Jimmy just happened to find the box Mr. Graves kept his spice cards in.

"According to the employees who knew," they soon learned that Jimmy was trying to manipulate the owner into giving the idiot a Ten Dollar Raise. And if he didn't, the young man was going to accuse his employer of sexual harassment.

When that did not work, Jimmy decided to go for the gold and was willing to Threaten Graves with the He Raped Me Routine.

If you were to listen to those that he bragged to, Mr. Bowen had a building picked out and was just waiting on the bank to get Graves cosigned signature added to the already approved loan.

Then a few days after Joyfully Gloating how much power he had over the old man, Jimmy Bowen never showed up to work again.

Being the Extreme Meth head that he was, "with a horrible work record to prove it," we all just assumed that Bowen was on another bender, and who knew if we would ever see him again that next day or any other day after that.

Jimmy Bowen was just that way.

Here today and gone tomorrow.

Later, after Arapahoe's Department of Investigation successfully captured S.S.K, Mr. Bowens unexpected and dated skin sample slide will be found amongst many others.

Its date will be listed as One slash Two slash Zero slash Three slash Nine slash Four.

As Jarrett entered Graves Meat Market and Deli, once again the Overpowering smells of meat took their hypnotic control over the Detective and every other unassuming customer that shopped at the Marketplace.

And since JJ had a little time on his hands, this visit would be done at a more leisurely pace.

He wanted to make sure this time that he made a list of all the Mouthwatering Products that were found inside this Willy Wonka place of Delectable Meats.

Today's Special even included one of JJ's Favorite types of flavored links.

Blood Sausage.

That Two Pound order was quickly placed while Jarrett continued to look around for other past and rarely recreated Masterpieces. The sight of Fresh Head Cheese was his next choice that would be accompanying Mr. Jefferson home.

Just the thought of that extra fattiness melting in his mouth, made the Detectives tongue water that much more.

Some of that Ground Hamburger meat would also be going home with him.

The spice flavor had been so Right On The Money, that JJ shared half of what he bought last time with a few of the other officers back at the department.

While the Detective finished placing his To Go order, a sandwich on the Deli's Hot and Fresh menu caught Jarrett's eye. Today's Special was a Hot Italian that came with Prosciutto, Salami, Spanish Chorizo, Pancetta and Pastrami.

Every Italians Last Dying wish, before they are all killed from a Heart Attack brought on by processed meats.

The only way to go, JJ's Italian Grandfather would always Profess.

MAMMA MIA.

CHE!

PANINO!

Grandfather would have Loved One or Two side orders consisting of those Vixen Goddesses who stroll topless down the sun lit Mediterranean beaches too; but at his age, those young Hot To Trot Beauties would just laugh him off as they giggly stroked his stubbled chin like some cute and lost pet.

That is when his story and wishes for the girls always ended the same way.

PRENDILA IN CULO DA UN CIUCCIO

IMBIZZARRITO, STRONZAS.

I would rather wrap a sandwich around my willy and go that way, then give them the universal keys to what a proper orgasm should look and feel like.

Bitches.

Bitches!

BITCHES!

Taking an unassuming seat over by one of the stores random walls, JJ could not help but see the humor in what Mr. Graves has done with his business.

Not Only did his selections of cured meats hang from every possible place that the ceiling could provide, but even the wall he was sitting next to had the markets Delicacies dripping from their flattened surfaces.

The Detective almost choked at the humor of it.

Mr. Graves was shoving his meat into the face of his customers.

And just like JJ, They Were Eating It Up.

As Officer Jarrett settled into the rhythm of bite, chew, then swallow, his attention soon began to focus on what was hanging amongst Mr. Graves Meaty Choices.

Accolade after accolade of articles and newspaper clippings honoring the man.

One of the largest write ups about his business came from the Denver Post.

The city was Declaring the Butcher a Local Icon do too the Many Years he has been serving the homeless community with his free donations of hamburger and sliced meats. It also seems that his Generosity was Not just contained to the counties that were considered a part of the Denver Metro..

The man's achievements were Nation Wide.

No matter where the need was at or what state it was from; if a Food Bank, Pantry, or shelter reached out to him for a supply of meat, he was more than willing to help those who asked.

When that time a bad case of the Corona Virus swept the states, "Including Colorado," he provided every school in the

Denver Metro and its surrounding counties with enough hamburger to feed an army.

The schools were also able to send the kids home with an extra burger for Both of their parents.

Many families would not have survived if it had not of been for Mr. Graves's Love and Generosity.

While JJ continued to gaze at picture frame after picture frame, it soon occurred to him that this man's hand was in every aspect of the public's personal lives.

Nursing homes, "Including those rich Senior Living Centers," have benefited from his Meaty Influences too.

More than one gathering dealing with either the Bridge Club, Church Function, Charity Event or Fund Raiser have had their parties served by his Market Place. Even the yearly ball at the Governor's Mansion was one of his Must Do catering jobs.

Those who ran The State of Colorado would not have had it any other way.

No wonder he's not able to track the owner down, Graves is a Very Busy Man.

Just as JJ was taking that last bite of his sandwich while heading to the pick-up counter, Becky from Dispatch was needing to get his attention.

Skinner may have struck again.

That guy he had talked with earlier from Mr. Bartholomew's business, was requesting a welfare check on an employee who was not responding to any of his messages. The elderly lady was consistent when it came to calling him back.

This lack of unprofessionalism was not like her.

And do to the elders advanced age and Unhealthy habits, she may have just fallen and injured herself.

Either way, he was hoping that you had some time to check in on her.

After receiving the location of One, Eight, Three, Two, Five, East Girard Avenue in Aurora, the department's Detective quickly jumped up and headed for his car. JJ never saw or heard the register girl trying to get his attention as he was walking out the door.

Their new employee Tammy was wanting to know if he would like a complimentary toothpick.

Their Cinnamon Flavored.

But Mr. Jefferson already had More Important things on his mind to worry about than a toothpick.

If the woman's absence was due to Skinner, it sounded as if the Frail Elder stood No Chance In Hell at any kind of self-defense if S.S.K. decided to bust down her door.

A busted door that he would soon be walking through.

Just as he was within a mile or so from Mile High's location, JJ just happened to see the man he was looking for.

Headed in the opposite direction from the scene Jarrett was needing to be, was Mr. Graves Red Nineteen Fifty-Three Dodge Panel Truck. The Antique vehicle looked freshly washed and the Custom Black Cherry paint job shouted out his eggshell colored name Loud and Proud.

Mr. Graves Market Place and Deli.

If You're a Carnivore,

Graves's Meats Will Satisfy That Craving.

One slash Seven slash Two slash Zero slash Eight slash Eight slash Eight slash Five slash Six slash One slash Two.

The way he had used the slash mark instead of the dash mark sent chills running down the Detective's spine. There was something just Way To Familiar about his phone number and how it had been written.

And then there were those other things about the vehicle which had caught Jarrett's attention also.

His business number was the Perfect match to the few digits his department currently had to work with.

That other suspicion Mr. Jefferson had earlier, quickly revealed itself once he realized that their welfare check ended up being Skinner's next crime scene. He and his red truck had Once Again been spotted in the area of a break-in that involved a missing person.

And the more JJ thinks about it, Mandy was doing her Damndest to say Graves.

It was at this point that Arapahoe's Detective wanted to turn around and pursue the possible killer, but that secure arrest would require a little more evidence.

Incriminating Documentation that had to be At Least Fifty Percent or More.

That's exactly what it would take to bring down a man of such standing amongst a community that not only has his back, but some of them would probably be willing to do whatever it took when it came to proving The Saint Of Meats innocents.

Colorado's Governor was just one of the hurdles that would be in need of jumping.

It was seeing the office door kicked in at JJ's first to the scene arrival, that caused the man to just put the car in park and give himself a moment to gather his busy thoughts.

Taking a Deep Breath before stepping out of his vehicle didn't hurt either.

Mr. Jefferson was going to need that steadiness just in case what was waiting to great him became overwhelming before his faculties could adjust.

With that first foot through the door, the Detective quickly noticed the Overwhelming smell of cigarettes in the Chainsmokers small studio apartment. And just like other Mile-High locations, the aroma of Cinnamon oil also permeated the thrashed and destroyed room.

And after seeing a personal picture of the woman framed upon the wall, JJ had no doubts that the elderly gal who looked like Sophia Petrillo from the Golden Girls did not go down without a fight.

Jefferson could be wrong; because her character was truly a spitfire, but the bottles of oxygen and breathing tubes said otherwise.

She Never stood a chance, he thought.

And what was waiting to greet him and the crime scene technicians in the refrigerator caused a unanimous agreement amongst everyone at the scene.

Skinner had taken another victim.

Virginia Trey Baker was Declared missing on Zero slash

Seven slash One slash Zero slash Three slash Zero.

That was also the day Jarrett Jefferson began to truly hate the commercials from Androids With Real Skin.

At AWRS, are you missing someone.

Because if you are, We Care.

When a picture or synthetic No Longer fills that void

We have the replacement for you.

Why Settle For

FAKE SKIN,

When You Can Have

REAL.

Look For A

REAL SKIN DEALER

Near You.

CH. 17
HELLO MOTHER.

Growing up, if Virginia's mom passed on any valuable life lessons to her; the abused woman showed the little girl how to take a punch. Mrs. Baker single handedly also taught her daughter how to fight back once that valuable lesson was experienced herself.

That life and death occurrence happened when Virginia was somewhere around Four or Five.

The little girl's daddy had come home from the bar drunk off his ass once again.

But this time, he didn't arrive alone.

The Confederate waiving redneck brought a few of his buddies from the oil rig with him also.

In fact, it was not just a few.

Daddy came home with Five other rig hands who worked the oil derrick with him.

He had promised the rough and tumble guys a gang bang with his wife.

And after Mr. Baker got his knuckled fist point across, the men dragged Momma into her and Daddy's Marriage bed and began to have their way with Virginia's Mother.

That drunken and against her will orgy went on for the entire Three Days the drug induced men were off.

As Little Virginia hid in her closet, the Testosterone induced sex fest almost put her mother in the hospital by the time daddy and his friends were through with his wife.

Since the liquor was producing that I Do not Give A Shit

Attitude Most Drunks Get, Daddy allowed the men to do whatever sexual acts they wanted with his Mrs. Baker. So long as she was still breathing and there was a vacant hole to be had, he would join in himself if the idea were kinky enough.

It was not until they were about to return to the rig that Momma had to find the courage to save them both.

If she hadn't, there's No Telling were the Two women would have ended up.

Mr. Baker's still intoxicated ass was wanting something a bit tighter than his wife's now wrecked vagina and was planning to take it from their little girl.

As the man stood stroking his cock over Virginia, Mrs. Baker had crawled her way into the kitchen. Calling out to God for the strength to do what was needed; that battered, and bleeding woman stood up and began swinging her Largest Cast Iron Skillet on the Son Of A Bitch.

The home wrecker never knew what hit him.

Mr. Graves experienced that same fury when he came at Virginia while she was doing her breathing treatment.

S.S.K. saw an easy catch, while his victim saw blood.

And that is exactly what the Crime Technicians found when they processed her scene.

Blood.

But this time, it was more than usual.

From the blood splatter to Virginia's chipped nails that were manicured on a weekly basis at Miss. Kim's Beauty Bar, at least a pint of the life-giving liquid was spread throughout the studio apartment.

And after a quick check of her medical records that were lying about, the A. Negative blood they were finding Was Not Hers.

It seems that Grandma had fought Skinner with everything she had.

But with her missing and now found skin sample slide in the refrigerator, everyone in the room understood the outcome that was awaiting the Great Grandmother.

She was now at the mercy of Arapahoe's Serial Killer.

S.S.K.

JJ was just about to ask if that was everything in the Ice Box; but before he could, the guy inspecting the food container said yours is here too Detective.

Skinner wanted to Make Sure JJ understood that his day was still at hand.

Even the date was exactly the same.

Three slash Zero.

As the situation's seriousness settled amongst the Detective, Virginia's nightmare was about to start.

The Seventy-Six-year-old woman was in the process of awakening inside Skinner's holding cage.

Her nude body quickly told the frail woman that she was laying chained to a concrete floor. The Extremely bright lights that filled her portion of the warehouse was making it almost impossible to focus.

Not having her glasses was not helping the situation either.

That is also when she noticed her wig was missing too.

While her cataracted eyes did their best to focus on her surroundings, the light boxes hanging on the walls were not helping the elders Were The Fuck Am I situation. But the voice that spoke from the overly lit room, reminded the gal that she knew Exactly who it was that had busted their way into her small apartment.

It was Mr. Graves from the Meat Market.

Her Favorite place to get Liverwurst and Limburger Cheese.

There was something about his Liverwurst that ticked the tock on her aging pallet.

Most people who were just lucky enough to reach their golden years tend to have a taste bud issue.

That's why she Loved the processed meat.

Its flavorful strength was strong enough to give her Nicotine Damaged Saliva Glands something to talk about.

And if she Just So Happens to survive what was about to happen, she would have Plenty to discuss until her last and dying days over another sandwich from his store.

Except, today would end up being that last and dying day.

S.S.K. was going to make sure of it.

Especially after what Miss. Baker did to his face.

Mr. Graves actually thought that the old lady sitting in her recliner was going to be his easiest mark yet, but her solid claws said otherwise. She almost peeled off the entire right side of Graves face before he was able to drug the victim.

Her vicious counterattack had broken every nail from the woman's left hand.

Skinner even had to do a little bit of surgery on himself after one of the dammed things broke off inside his cheek bed.

The Serial Killer had no doubt that they Officially had his DNA now.

As Miss. Baker laid inside the cage, the elderly woman began to realize that the bondage situation she was currently subdued in was never going to allow her a chance at escaping.

She was here to stay and nothing, "unless a Golam just happened to show up," was going to save her from what was about to happen next.

S.S.K. was wanting to play and she was the game piece he would be experimenting with.

Through trial and error, her captor quickly began to realize that the skin on Really Old People tended to get damaged as he tried to Deskin them.

Their extreme and deep wrinkles always got in the way.

Also, it usually ripped from being So Thin.

And tobacco users were The Worst.

The dermatitis on geriatric smokers tended to be paper thin.

It was right about then; Skinner had an idea for a new line of products for his store.

Not only could he use their skins to start a stationary line of homemade and one of a kind paper, but their bodies are usually filled with prescription drugs and nicotine, if not alcohol too. That disposing of a chemically filled body on the verge of embalmment would have to be dealt with in a completely different manner

Using their flesh, he could create a doggie treat section that offered CBD qualities for a person's pet pooch.

A drug inducing dog cookie that can be used to calm an overly active animal.

Skinner even found it amusing enough to loudly laugh at the prospect of saying that they were Safe for children too.

As her out of focus butcher stepped into the room, S.S.K. grabbed the woman by her chain and then proceeded to have an unrealistic conversation with Miss. Baker about that one time she So Reminded Bill of his mother.

The elderly lady had scooted her way into his store with a lit cigarette in one hand and her portable oxygen tank in the other. That day was one of the times Mr. Graves just happened to still be on the premises after opening.

He didn't know whether to be Appalled or Overly Concerned at that moment.

Graves pissed off response after telling Virginia to put that thing out before she contaminated his meat, was not the greeting she was expecting. Neither was his second command well received when Mr. Graves gave her the order to, DO IT NOW Before You Blow Us All To Kingdom Come.

It was Miss. Baker's FUCK YOU response which ended up getting her band from His Store for the rest of her Soon-To-- Be shortened life.

Skinner never really planned to harvest the bitch do to her age but seeing her sitting so defenseless in the chair at Mile High, turned out to be one of those wonderful and unexpected bonuses life tends to randomly toss a person's way now and then.

And Now, Skinner was going to take every advantage he had with the old bitty and use her confinement as a time of experimentation.

Instead of choosing the scalpel to deskin her, he was wondering if an air hose would be better.

If he could pump her underlying layer full of air, the skin just might stretch back out to where he wouldn't damage her outer layer while it was being removed.

And do to its poor condition, no one would ever buy it from him anyway.

That is why his new line of products for the store made Perfect Sense.

Waste Not Want Not, has always been his motto.

Especially after his First Kills.

His parents John and Ruth Graves never saw him coming. And neither did he at first.

After selling their house and business, the couple made it Very Clear that they were moving, and he Was not welcomed to join them. This proclamation had been made after Bill realized that they Never Did mention or acknowledge him in the Denver Post's article about their retirement.

Confronting them over why there was no mentioning of his name, the elderly couple commented that they No Longer had a son.

Bill would later learn that his parents had stricken his name from every family record.

Not one mention of his existence could be found.

If they did have a son, he would never have turned into a pot head like the man sitting in front of them currently is. It was just soon afterwards that Bill found out that his name had been removed from their Last Will and Testament also.

That was the day their son snapped.

It was also the day they unknowingly went missing too.

Zero slash Three slash Two slash One slash Eight slash Zero.

As the morphine continued to run its course through Virginia's frail body, an Overpowering smell of cinnamon invaded the cage just as its door was getting unlocked.

Being the tiny woman that she was, Skinner never had to drag or use the electric wench to place her body upon his carving table. He just grabbed the chain and carried Miss. Baker like a suitcase.

Her Sixty-pound frame was a breeze to the Very Stout Butcher.

While her crumpled body was being strapped to his table, Miss. Baker groggily asked him why he was doing this. His; YOUR JUST LIKE MY MOTHER response, sent chills down the woman's already hypothermic leaning body.

It appears as if he had a grudge with his momma and Virginia quickly understood that this situation was not going to end well for her now.

That, and he had recognized her from their shouting match in his store awhile back.

Seems the man also has an issue with forgiveness.

Just how deep that hatred went was soon to be experienced by Skinner's current victim.

After rolling over a compressor tank and its set of multiple hoses; All fitted with that thick Industrial Sized needle used for airing up things like footballs, basketballs, and volleyballs, S.S.K. began to puncture Virginia's outer shell with the implements.

He then proceeded to start the process of inflating her skin.

Since it's always easier to work his way up, "because his captives tended to live longer," Mr. Graves took his own sweet time to enjoy the artistic quality of his latest trial and error project. Her FUCK YOU RESPONSE last time they met was another reason he was so pleasantly pleased to take his time.

This Bitch Needed To Suffer.

Placing the compressor on its lowest setting, Mr. Graves went to the next step of his process.

Those extra ingredients needed for making doggie treats.

Whistling a favorite tune from his youth, "How Much Is That Doggie In The Window," the Butcher started cleaning the meat grinder that Virginia's chemically infused body would be ground through.

S.S.K. had also decided to turn her leathery skin into products that resembled freeze dried pig ears.

He was Absolutely Certain that the dogs were going to love them.

It was also right about then that Mr. Graves remembered one of the woman's Favorite products.

Liverwurst.

He was willing to bet that the liver her body used to filter the poisons from Virginia's living carcass would give the product a nice bite of harshness.

It seems that when it came to Meat Standards, the Stronger the Bite the Better was preferred by the elderly who were usually the Only Ones willing to purchase the processed product. And most of those who Loved the shit, were more than likely to have been born or raised during Germany's War.

Taking the chance that he may be right; Mr. Graves grabbed the now SCREAMING woman by the wrist as he began to search for that specific identification of a Jew during the time of Hitler.

And he found it; just as Victoria began to spit out the words Linux Nazi, Linux Nazi, Linux Nazi between her SCREAMS and FUCK YOU Responses.

S.S.K. did have to give the Old Bat some credit though. Its been awhile since he's had a Hell Cat such as this.

As the inflation of Miss. Baker's body began to reach her waist, Skinner was pleasantly surprised to see that her shell casing was holding itself together.

That questionability of why, came as a bonus when he realized that there would be lots of extra skin when it came time to make the chewy freeze-dried treats. Seems Victoria had been Severely Overweight in her earlier years and now all of that Extra Skin would be put to beneficial use.

Every last pound of it.

One of those unexpected surprises about her demise happened just as the air finally reached Miss. Baker's fingers, the arthritic structures popped right out of their skinned containments.

Skinner thought that the inflating method would more than likely stop once the air reached her neck and skintight skull, but it didn't. With a little bit of pressure applied manipulation, Virginia Baker quickly began to resemble her teenage self, back during those days of overly bloated plumpness.

Even her cheeks and lips took on that Collagen appearance everyone in Beverly Hills seems to have and want these days.

The last thing the widowed Baker visually heard before the darkness over took her, was the busting sound of a balloon as the final portions of her skin ripped from the old woman's face.

POP!

Turned out, she was the easiest deskinning that he has ever had.

Something S.S.K. was Definitely going to try on a firmer carcass.

Maybe the Detective, "if he was Lucky Enough," could be the next one to test out Mr. Graves newly discovered method of skin from meat separation.

They just needed to connect somehow, and that gathering, "Unbeknownst to Mr. Graves," would be here before Skinner new it. And while he contemplated that fateful day; the Killer's Employer, "Androids with Real Skin," began to play their latest Ad across the public airwaves of Denver's Radio and Television Stations.

Here at AWRS, We Care About You and Your Health.

That is why we have stopped making Latex Synthetics.

What good is a Latex Android if those who are allergic to them cannot use or touch one.

It's Time For That Atrocity To End.

Why Settle For

FAKE SKIN,

When You Can Have

REAL.

Look For A

REAL SKIN DEALER

Near You.

CH. 18
WE'VE ALREADY MET.

As the sun began to rise on day Eleven, JJ was starting to suspect that the key to everything concerning their Serial Killer S.S.K. was connected to that pay phone at Graves's Meat Market and Deli.

He was Sure Of It.

That's why he was here this morning right as the doors were being unlocked for their breakfast run.

He Needed to talk with the Owner.

But as luck would have it, Mr. Graves had already left and was busy making the days deliveries.

And after Almost pissing off the clerk and those waiting in line behind the Detective with All of his Persistent questions, JJ was given the choice to place his order Right Now or Leave.

The fresh smell of fried Liverwurst on the hot grill settled which answer he was going to give as to the action he was being ordered to make. I will take a fried liverwurst sandwich with EXTRA Hot White onion and some melted Limburger Cheese on Sharpened Dark Rye Bread.

His follow-up: and a diet coke too, got a slight chuckle from those standing behind Mr. Jefferson.

The Hot gal a few customers back, wanted to know if Jarrett was watching his figure.

Their simultaneous laughing response ended up getting the Detective something he has not received in a Long, Long time.

A strange woman's phone number.

Graves's Business number that was Seventy Percent

Identical to the one they were searching for, was one of the Reason's JJ was here too. There were Way Too Many Coincidences that were starting to pop up concerning the owner and S.S.K.

As Jarrett slipped down one of his rabbit holes, he subconsciously began to count the number of times this has happened.

He had the Last Same Name as the Now Missing John and Ruth Graves.

His Delivery Van has now been seen around More Than One Crime Scene.

The phone number associated with the missing was listed as belonging to the pay phone outside his business.

And then there was his unaccountability, "while out making deliveries," of just where he was at, while the attacks were occurring.

It wasn't until the Dementia acting guy's tray was slammed down onto the table from a disgruntled employee, that JJ finally returned to reality. Seems the disheveled and want Not To Be A Waiter had been calling his name over their Your Order Is Ready intercom.

Three Fucking Times was his mumbled conversation as the employee walked away.

With the smell of Mouth-Watering Putridness invading the Detective's nostrils, JJ picked up his sandwich and took the largest bite those watching him had ever seen.

Well that's Just an Inappropriate smell, was one of many whispered responses.

The next set of vocalization comments were due to what was on his plate.

Not only had the Pissed Off waiter gotten everyone's attention, but the realization of what the man was about to eat had most eyes locked onto his next move.

JJ took another willing bite from the skunkish sandwich.

A smell that by this time had invaded every corner of the Market's dining room.

While JJ was overtaken by the elixir of Liverwurst,

Limburger Cheese, Hot White Onion and Stone Ground Mustard that had all been piled on Freshly Baked Rye Bread, his clouded gaze of contentment began to unconsciously scan the eating room for more articles concerning Mr. Graves.

He was also lost in trying to decipher just what that extra spark in the Liverwurst was.

The unknown spice was tantalizingly tickling his taste buds.

Just like the newly discovered articles hanging from the walls were doing for Jefferson's inquisitiveness. It seems that the last time Arapahoe's Detective had been here, he somehow missed the section that contained photographs of his mystery suspect.

The First photo JJ noticed was a black and white print taken of a Much Younger Man standing next to his Nineteen Fifty-Three Dodge Panel Truck. And even though it looked as if Thirty Years have now passed, Mr. Jefferson Suddenly realized that he actually recognized the man in the picture.

It was Bill Graves.

The last person that saw, helped, and spoke with his wife.

That's when JJ heard the Southern portion of his Louisiana Spirit shout out that the Coon-ass's bowl of Gas Inducing beans were ready to be slurped and slopped.

Bill Graves just may be the Serial Killer they have been searching for.

S.S.K.

That kind of Wonderful Announcement in the South always came with Cornbread and Butter Too.

Tearing out of the business's parking lot, JJ understood that he Immediately needed to get back and search his notes at the Department.

Somewhere in Jeans' cold case file was the address associated with the man Jarrett Now wanted to have a talk with. He also needed to figure out where the missing people and their bodies were.

There's No Way Around It, He must be doing something with them.

The thought did pop into Mr. Jefferson's head that the man did own a Meat Market.

That would be The Perfect Place to dispose of all Evidence.

JJ's guts almost wrenched this morning's meal as he tried to suppress the Horrible and Unthinkable idea.

Graves would not actually do that, would he.

While those back at the station Quizzedly watched the man run through the front doors as if the Undead were chasing him, JJ's frazzled hurriedness caused the Detective to forget that he needed to check in his gun first.

The small hallway that scanned for weapons went into automatic lock down as he tried to open that second door.

It took some serious convincing that he was not here to play a game of let's Go Postal, before Dutch finally felt safe enough to release him. JJ's haggard and out of breath response of OPEN THIS FUCKING DOOR, was not helping his Parole matters though.

What did set the Detective free was when he shouted to the Chief that He Knows Who S.S.K. is.

Handing over His Mag 9 between the slightly cracked door, Jarrett was finally let into the Department's Main Investigation room.

Almost knocking those over who had taken up a viewing and response stance of just in case something did go wrong; Jefferson literally knocked his best friend John Randal to the ground as he sprinted for the storage area where cold case files were kept.

Jean's were still in the exact same spot were JJ last hid them.

In the paneled ceiling right above his working head.

Hurriedly grabbing the box and dropping back down to his desk, Dutch was almost sent reeling against the far wall as JJ's Falling Ass took out the man who had come to help him down.

Just to sniff that Virgin Butt Crack was Well Worth It, Daddy Rob told his Little Piggy, Piggy Pete later that evening. Something Dutch learned a few days after His Boy Toy came clean about his and JJ's Mall excursion.

Thankfully His: What The Hell JJ Response, Instantly covered Any and All Willful signs of Ill, Malicious or Sexual Attempt on the Chiefs behalf.

Dutch's next question quickly changed the subject before Randal had a chance of creating that next Crude, Unacceptable and Always Permanent work joke. One about him and JJ that would end up haunting these premises Long After they are Both Gone.

Not something he was going to allow John an opportunity to achieve.

Tell us what you found Detective.

If Mr. Graves was the last person to have seen and talked with his wife; Jarrett pointed out, then this means Jean Did not Leave Him.

She's!

Actually!

Missing!

That's also when a realization of unthinkable proportions hit the widowed husband.

Skinner might have killed her too.

So Far, Mrs. Jefferson's skin sample hasn't been found amongst all the others.

And JJ was keeping his fingers crossed that it never would.

As he blindly ripped through the box containing Rollins and Thomas's investigation, the Detective's heart began to sink when he couldn't find any trace of Mr. Graves's interview, address, or any kind of vehicle ownership at that time.

It seems that information was some of the evidence that had either been destroyed or manipulated.

JJ's SCREAMS OF HELL NO and THOSE MOTHER FUCKING ASSHOLES Quickly regained everyone's attention in the room.

Most everyone knew what had occurred between Jarrett and the Two Officers who had disgraced themselves and Arapahoe's office of investigation. They also knew that corroborating material that would have Instantly exonerated JJ at the time had been destroyed too.

That's why they are No Longer working here.

Remembering the county that had been willing to accept their applications, JJ instantly picked up the phone and began to dial the Sherriff's Office in Montezuma County. And after a breathless and Angered explanation of why he was calling and who it was that he Was Needing to speak with, their response sent the man Reeling.

Both Men went missing last night.

Their patrol vehicle was found abandoned on a rarely used dirt road West of Cortez.

Somewhere near Highline ditch.

That's just over One Mile East of Totten lake.

It seems the Two Deputies had walked into an unexpected ambush.

An unknown caller had reached out to report that a group of kids were out drinking and either setting off fireworks or they possibly had a gun. To keep the few residents out that way safe, Roland and Vance were sent to investigate.

When they never checked back in, another patrol car was sent out and their abandoned vehicle was found about Two Hours later.

They However Were Not.

As this Major setback started to slightly unravel JJ, the county's Chief Officer said something that sent shivers of Iced Death Roaring down Jarrett's spine.

We did find something odd though, Detective.

There were Two Skin Sample Slides inside of Thomas's lunch box.

We are just not sure what to make out of them yet.

With a quick thank you; before slamming the phone down, Mr. Jefferson went racing into Dutch's office unannounced.

That dumb ass move got him a Boisterous Reprimand, until he spoke those Three Magical Words.

Skinner's Struck Again.

While JJ stood their looking at his chief with a Trembling and Soon To Be OUTRAGED Response for a reprimand, Dutch calmly started speaking to his Frazzled Detective.

He has Unexpected News.

It seems that not only had some of the missing evidence been recovered concerning Jean's cold case, but the department had also recorded a confession from both men before they were sent packing.

Once those revelations were revealed, JJ's Anger EXPLODED upon the man who was his Superior.

WHY WAS THIS NEVER TOLD TO HIM!

WHY ARE THESE THINGS NOT IN JEAN'S CASE FILE!

WHERE ARE THE RECORDINGS NOW!

AND, WHY THE HELL WAS DUTCH STILL SITTING ON HIS LAZY ASS INSTEAD OF HANDING HIM THIS INFORMATION RIGHT FUCKING NOW!

When it came to the department's change on who could and who was not allowed to have a gun past the main entry into this part of their investigation area, The Chief had been the one who was responsible for making that final decision.

And that announcement concerning who would have such a Second Amendment right, included the Department's Lieutenant.

Chief Rob Dutch.

As JJ began to Shake His Fist While Ranting and Raving at Dutch, Rob inconspicuously lowered his hand down to the gun's butted end and slowly started to unbuckle his weapon.

If Jarrett even looked as if he were about to consider tearing Dutch's office apart like he did last time, the man had No Qualms about shoving the barreled end of the weapon down Detective Jefferson's throat.

After that time with Pete in the men's room, Rob has always wondered what it would feel like to force something long and hard into JJ's mouth.

All he was needing was an opportunity and a reason.

Would this be the day?

They were both about to find out.

But with everything already going on, Dutch would not be getting his Make-A-Wish Hopes fulfilled today or any other day.

Seeing his hand slowly slide down to his side was enough of a deterrent to make Jarrett take a deep breath as the Detective forced himself to calm his Fucking Ass Down.

Today was the day he needed Dutch as an ally and not his enemy.

This would also turn out to be the day Arapahoe's Department of Investigation Finally got a lead on their suspect The Skin Sample Killer, or Skinner as everyone else on the case eventually came to call the man now known as Bill Graves.

While JJ tore through the latest paperwork looking for Graves last known address that had been, "ACCIDENTLY," misplaced and forgotten, an All-Points Bulletin was put out for his vehicle.

A Nineteen Fifty-Three Dodge Panel Truck with No Side Windows.

The vehicle's color was listed as Black Cherry.

And the License plate came back as S for Snake, K for Kids, I for Ingrate, N for Nancy, N for Nancy, E for Ed, and R for Roy.

Or, SKINNER for short.

It seems that Mr. Graves had seen in the Denver Post that the Serial Killer S.S.K. was given the nickname Skinner.

And He Liked It.

Mr. Graves Liked It So Much, that the vehicles newly personalized plate had just recently been changed.

And that's also when JJ struck Pay Dirt, they had a current address associated with the plate.

Keeping his fingers crossed that the address wasn't attached to a vacant lot or a Post Office Box, the gal at their Department of Transportation began to sound out the location of where the owner should be found.

Two, One, Four, Seven, Eight, East Mansfield Place.

If JJ had not of been in such a hurry, "before he slammed the phone down," the Record Keeper would also have given him an older address that was located out East, just off Quincy Avenue and Bennett Road.

Four, Seven, Six, Six, Eight, Airline Road.

The Exact Location Rollins and Thomas were being held by

the man who had jumped them last night as they were out doing a routine check west of Cortez.

Someone had called in about a group of rowdy kids causing property damage.

Neither officer was expecting to find an elderly man in a Really Old Van Like Truck waiting to ambush them.

As Rollins ordered Thomas to go and see if anyone was in the abandoned looking vehicle, he was going to take a piss before joining him. The man wasn't even able to shake it twice, when the scuffle taking place inside the vehicle quickly caught his attention.

The lack of response from Vance after Roland called out his name sent his partner into overdrive.

Something Was Wrong.

Sadly, Rollins's hyped up testosterone response ended before he was able to reach for his service weapon.

The tranquilizer syringe of morphine that was thrown first, struck its target better than any bulls eyed dart ever thrown in a bar or tournament. Roland reaching up and accidently hitting the plunger had not done the man any favors either.

He instantly went down like a Ten Dollar whore who was late and supposed to have met and payed her Pimp over Twenty Minutes Ago.

While Skinner began to load the second officer into his Delivery Truck, S.S.K. couldn't believe his luck. The only Two people who could expose his identity, were now his captives and on their way to the warehouse.

Once Mr. Graves realized that the woman he had taken from the bank was a Detective's Wife, the Butcher began to watch her missing case a little more intensely than All Other news media stories.

The Meat Market Owner was also paying attention when Detective Jarrett Jefferson had been exonerated after it was revealed that the Two Officers in charge of his case had, "Not Only," been reprimanded for mismanagement of evidence, but they were also accused of biasness towards JJ.

And after finding a Googled article about them being on the

radar, "Once Again," for actions Unbecoming of an Officer, S.S.K. Was Certain that No One would miss the Pair.

And he was Absolutely right.

The lack of response to their disappearance began that very day they were declared missing.

Zero slash Seven slash One slash One slash Three slash Zero.

CH. 19
HERE KILLER, KILLER.

While Detective Jarrett sprinted to his car, the two captured officers were unwillingly locked in a race of their own.

A Life and Death event that was looking increasingly like a sprint instead of a Marathon.

But they were not just wrong; Rollins and Thomas were going to be DEAD WRONG. The Two Former Detectives had tried to destroy that which belonged to Skinner, And Only Skinner.

A Mr. Jarrett S. Jefferson.

Due to The Idiots putting their noses in someone else's Damned business, Skinner's taste for officers had grown Extremely Distasteful.

He was going to take his Sweet, Sweet Time on these Two.

Their Intrusion into His Life had Not Only costed the man his Nineteen Eighties Trophy Case,

But, He Also Lost One Thousand and Twenty skin sample slides that day.

Two of those microscope plates belonged to his Mom and Dad, John, and Ruth Graves.

They even took the one thing that his parents claimed As Theirs, before trying to sell it.

HIS CHAIR!

When Mom and Pop Graves revealed that they were selling the chair from the cutting station he had been working at for close to Twelve Years, Bills' falling on deaf ears OUTRAGE set Mr. and Mrs. Graves doomsday clocks into motion.

Kind of like what was now occurring to the Two missing men.

Their personal knowledge about him and were he could be found turned out to be the tock that ticked their demise.

They Just Knew TOO MUCH.

So, as Skinner began to collect his missing One Thousand and Twenty skin samples from Rollins's strapped down and drug induced body, Jarrett was arriving at the home address associated with Mr. Graves.

As JJ pulled into the two-story homes triple car garaged driveway, he was surprised to see such a manicured lawn.

With the man supposedly being single and quite possibly working Twenty-Four Hours a day, Seven Days A Week; it seems the Half a Million Dollar structure was in great shape. Every board and splash of paint was picture perfect.

A True Standout amongst its neighborhood competitors.

Creeping up to the built-in porch with its single-entry door, Detective Jarrett did his best to inconspicuously peer into the first and only window on his left.

That view turned out to be a Complete Disappointment.

A walled in dining room with no conceivable way of seeing into the rest of Graves house stared back at JJ. The Two side by side single windows that were to the far right of the houses front door looked down a long and empty hallway.

With the double garage doors closed and it still being mid-day, Graves was More Than Likely Not Home.

JJ was willing to bet that he was probably still out and making deliveries.

That deduction was why Detective Jefferson decided to jump the side gate and take a look around back.

That view: do to its Many Windows, answered JJ's main question.

No one was home.

And even though it was a bachelor pad of an elderly man, its spotlessness and museum quality look gave the appearance that no one has lived at this location for quite a while.

Most everything within view looked as if it hasn't been

dusted in years though.

Jarrett thought that was really sad after seeing Mr. Graves beautiful lawn.

It seemed that this lead was turning out to be nothing more than a Total Bust and a Complete Waste Of Time.

The thing to do now was either head back to the Office, Drive around town searching for the vehicle or head on back to his Favorite Meat Market and hope that Graves just happens to show up.

That third choice might actually be the Perfect choice.

Where better to catch a killer than at his place of business.

JJ began to think that there's always a chance the owner may have forgotten something. There was even a possibility that this would be the day Mr. Graves just happened to run short on one of his specials and had No Other Choice but to swing back by to restock the truck.

Either way, Jarrett was starving and ready for something to eat.

Being just a little past One in the afternoon, Skinner realized that he was getting hungry too.

This time would also make a Great Opportunity for his guest to see just where they were going to end up.

Violently Slapping Roland's face after setting him chin up and face forward, S.S.K. quickly got the cops full attention. Mr. Graves was hungry and wanted to show the man what They were going to eat for Lunch.

Hamburgers.

And since Thomas was still chained up in the cage and unable to see what was making the grinding sound, he had to rely on Rollins's revealing SCREAMS that the unrecognizable noise was not worth seeing or knowing about.

As the Detectives bald and strapped down head watched the killer, Mr. Graves flipped on the meat grinder and began to insert someone's entire forearm.

That part was not as shocking to Skinner's captive until the Butcher took his one man show to the next level. After lighting a gas burner and placing Virginia Baker's Extra-Large Cast-iron frying pan on the stove, S.S.K. reached into the ground meat and started forming some hamburger patties for Himself, Roland, and Vance.

That realization of Guess What's For Lunch was the reason for Another SCREAM to ROAR from the bound officer.

His next HORRIFYING SCREAM came during another revelation.

Not Only did the blue tub look like the same style of container meat was served from at Mr. Graves store, "but if it was," it was the same meat Rolland was buying and using when friends and family were invited over for a weekend barbeque.

That third SCREAM came when the bound man suddenly understood why no victims have ever been found.

The Department has been looking in All The Wrong Places.

Skinner's been feeding his victims to Not Only Denver's Homeless Shelters, But His Customers TOO.

Rollins did not want to accept that fact, but all the smoked and drying meat selections hanging from the racks, ceiling and walls said otherwise.

And just as Roland began to drown in the depths of that horror, the bound man had another epiphany.

Graves Meat Market has been in business almost Fifty Years.

It Looks as if he started during the Exact Decade his skin samples at their crime scene were dated.

THE EIGHTIES!

Eighty also turned out to be the speed JJ's Heavy Nascar Foot had settled on as he raced to get himself some late lunch.

Every minute that he was on the road, another valuable second may get missed looking for Mr. Graves whereabouts. His business was having a special today and JJ hoped that he wouldn't miss out on that too.

Cheeseburgers.

These things were Not Only a step above a Juicy Lucy, Their overly filled cheese centers were what gave birth to Lucy.

Today Mamacita, "or Hot Mama," would be joining JJ for

Lunch.

This One Pound Behemoth turned out to be All That and So Much More.

Especially after Arapahoe County's Investigative Team Broke the Case On S.S.K. and exactly what was in Mr. Graves Extremely Sought-After Meats.

While JJ was waiting for his Medium-Rare burger to cook, the Detective began to do the one thing he was Really Good At, JJ continued snooping amongst the pictures that were hidden within the wall's hanging meats.

Something several customers were Not Pleased With, as the Detective's Didn't Give A Shit attitude about Their Whiny Feelings intrusively invaded Their Personal and Private space.

Ninety percent of the framed mementos were nothing but article after article praising the man for feeding Not Only The Public, but The Homeless Too.

Every now and then, another picture of Mr. Graves could be found here or there.

Arapahoe's Detective would and could have spent hours going over the possible evidence, but his burger was finally ready.

And so was the grumble in his empty stomach that was calling for the Fresh Fried Meat.

Getting lost down another rabbit hole after taking his first bite, JJ almost swallowed the larger than usual piece of gristle that had escaped the grinding machine. That showstopper of getting lost in one's imagination was quickly halted by the bluish tinted piece of bone that was unchewable.

And lucky for Mr. Jefferson, it did.

His unfettered gaze slowly began to focus on a picture that had somehow escaped his gaze.

Mr. Graves was standing next to his parked truck by some tin shed that looked as if it needed to be demolished.

The perfect place to subdue and kill someone, JJ thought.

Its abandoned and in the middle of Nowhere looking location, would have been the exact place Jarrett might have chosen if he himself just happened to be in the business of killing.

And that is when the Detective Quickly Realized where He Needed to be.

Graves hidden warehouse.

Where it was located at was another matter.

So that he could finish his burger out in the car, JJ went ahead and asked for a to-go box. He also made sure to report what may have been someone's fingernail in his burger.

This time around: before he could walk out the Deli, a small complimentary box of Candy consisting of Red Hots, was given to him so that JJ could cleanse his pallet. The small Cinnamon looking breath mints would help disguise his onion smelling breath.

Another Oddity, "associated with All their crime scenes," that was now stacking up as evidence against Mr. Graves.

As he sat in his car, JJ Decided to give The Department of Transportation another try.

The Officer was Quite Surprised when the same gal he talked with earlier just happened to pick up the phone.

And after remembering his Rude Ass and the way JJ had slammed down the phone on her before she was done giving Mr. Jefferson all the information that he had been asking for, the spiteful employee Almost decided to repay him with the same kindness.

But as of this moment, it was one of those days she couldn't.

They were under evaluation and the Department's Supervisor just happened to be standing at her station, Right Fucking Now.

Trying to be the perfect and cordial employee, the still fuming woman explained that she could have given him the address earlier, but He Hung Up before it was possible. Asking JJ if he would like it now, "with a disgruntled voice colder than death," he thankfully said yes to her invite.

The man known as Mr. Graves had a second building listed as private property.

Its address was located at Forty-Seven Thousand, Six Hundred and Sixty-Eight Airline Road.

And that's when JJ lost any chance of asking the single mother out on any kind of date, he Once Again hung up on the gal without thanking Barb for her valuable time.

Her Fuck You Too Asshole response, ended up giving the DOT's Employee a black mark reprimand on her evaluation that day. Something she would repay him for, by sending Mr. Jefferson a bouquet of stinging needles and poison ivy that following week.

She and Many of her scorned girlfriends just happened to know a place.

As JJ began to head out of dodge, he also made sure to call the Department's Chief of Investigation.

With this location possibly being dangerous, Dutch agreed with his Detective that any and all backup would be highly appropriate at this time. He was also Warning Jarrett Not to go all John Wayne.

Jefferson needed to wait until backup arrived before approaching the possible crime scene.

But as with all good officers, that order went in one ear and Right Out the other.

Even though Rollins and Thomas were Jarrett's Sworn Enemies; they were only taken last night.

There's an actual chance that Both Officers might still be alive.

JJ almost couldn't believe that he was considering his response and their lives to a Fate tossed chance of a coin. Seems that the God's were on Rolland and Vance's side that day.

His should or shouldn't I intervention toss, ended up heads I will.

The outcome to that game of randomness, almost didn't manifest once JJ headed out East on Quincy Avenue.

It seems that Airline Road was not a county or maintained option.

The barely visible dirt track was private and severely unmaintained.

Graves street address also turned out to be one of those

rare, hidden and Almost Impossible to Find roadways that were only marked by a Two-Inch-wide by Twelve-inch piece of numbered plastic.

It wasn't until the Detective started stopping and looking at every dirt road along the avenue, that he finally discovered the bent, twisted and severely weathered sign. Jarrett was pretty pissed when he realized that he had already driven bye, "and back bye," the land locator at least Three Times Now.

What a Stupid Son Of A Bitch was the man's self-response to his inattentiveness.

Time was of the Essence now, and there was not any Room for Fuck-up's JJ Proclaimed to himself.

Stupid.

STUPID.

STUPID!

Making sure to leave his parked patrol vehicle out by the main road where everyone else could find it, Mr. Jefferson began his keep your eyes on the prize track down the quiet and dirt road.

If anything were to go south at this point, the Detective understood that only his head would be rolling if things just happened to go Horribly Wrong.

Something he had No Problem living with right now.

JJ was ABSOLUTELY CERTAIN that lives were at stake.

And even though his alter ego of I Must Save The Day; wanted to sprint the remaining distance to the shed that was just beginning to show its rusted roof top from behind the hill, Jarrett's self-preservation knew better.

Skinner may have the place and its surrounding plot Booby Trapped.

Another price JJ was willing to pay if its end result meant bringing down the Serial Killer S.S.K.

It wasn't until the crouching Detective peaked over the hill top, that he suddenly realized that his luck had Finally changed.

JJ won the Lottery.

Skinner was home.

The **SCREAMS** that were reverberating from inside the shed also said that he wasn't alone.

Vance Thomas was begging for his Very Life.

It also seemed that Mr. Graves and his uncontrollable Laughter was enjoying the show, while the smell wafting through the air proclaimed that they were having hamburgers for lunch too.

JJ could still taste that wonderful elixir of meat upon his saliva glands, while the excitement of catching Skinner was causing the food moisteners in his mouth to drool as they desired another bite of his Delectable meat.

And of course, the blaring radio inside the tin shed was playing Skinner's song.

Here at Androids With Real Skin,
Our customers mean everything to us.
And when it comes to their kinks,
Those matter too.
If you have an oral fixation,
Plastic will Never Satisfy the tongue.
Why Settle For
FAKE SKIN,
When You Can Have
REAL.
Look For A
REAL SKIN DEALER
Near You.

CH. 20
WHERE'S THE BEEF.

As the law enforcement intruder neared the sheds front door, JJ was overly thankful after realizing that the blustery winds out on Colorado's easterly plains would easily aid in covering up any sounds he just happened to accidently make.

The wind machine's cranked-up effect was making the dilapidated looking structure creak and moan at their every wail.

Finally, fate seemed to be staying in JJ's corner.

She even began to smile on him more, when the detective realized that there weren't any windows that would betray his snooping around.

Jarrett almost shit his pants though, after slithering around the corner and right into the Panel trucks Unmovable left-front bumper.

His; That Mother Fucking Hurt Exclamation, frightened the Detective into thinking that he had just compromised himself. But, with no one busting out the front door; JJ slowly let out a quieted sigh of relief.

He let out another sigh after successfully slinking quietly through the buildings creaky front door.

That prayer turned out to be the first time Mr. Jefferson has had anything to do with God, since Jean went missing. If the Deity was All Knowing as the church professes, why didn't the man upstairs give her husband a heads up.

JJ had Two answers to that question before he walked away from his faith in God last year.

The guy either hates him or He Does not Exist.

No Matter What, JJ was Absolutely Certain that there would be No Divine Intervention on his Behalf today.

And His intuition could not have been more wrong.

If the Detective had been paying attention to his surroundings instead of the knee knocker that almost took him down, he would have seen Mr. Graves sitting in the driver's seat of his Nineteen Fifty-Three Dodge Panel Truck.

The man was just about to start its engine and leave, when JJ came slipping around the west side corner of his building.

Watching the Detective silently draw his gun just as he hobbled through the front door, seemed to give Skinner the motivation he was needing to stay. His afternoon deliveries would just have to either wait or be put off until tomorrow.

This opportunity was one that he was Not willing to pass up.

And neither was JJ.

He had a Killer to catch.

As Arapahoe's One-Manned Department of Investigation entered the L Shaped building, Mr. Jefferson was met with a bloodied and empty steel cage. The wall to his left, on his right and opposite of the front entrance door were covered from floor to ceiling in lit light boxes.

It appeared as if S.S.K. had been able to successfully recover his skin sample trophies from all the Mile-High Storage Facilities that had been ran by Bart and Beth Bartholomew.

But JJ had no time to dwell on that evidence.

Off to his left, upon the cross shaped table, was a strapped down Thomas.

The man appeared to be bathing in his own blood.

And that wasn't the worst of it.

When the armed Detective made his way safely over to the subdued man, Jarrett saw firsthand just why he was bleeding so much.

S.S.K. had used his and Roland's flesh to replace the One Thousand and Twenty Skin Sample Slides their department had taken into evidence almost Two Weeks Ago.

But, that wasn't even the shocking part.

That soul scaring jump came when JJ actually realized that Vance Thomas was still alive.

After Jarrett was hit by the Impacting Revelation that the bloodied victim was speaking to him, Mr. Jefferson quickly began to unbuckle his former acquaintance.

All the while, Skinner was silently watching and stalking his current prey from just outside the building's entrance. His opportunity to enter the structure sight unseen, finally happened when the Detective took notice of what was going on around the darkened corner.

Meat.

Lots.

And Lots.

Of meat.

As JJ started to unbuckle Vance's skinless feet, his conscious mind began to notice just how full the other room was. It held racks and racks of meat being cured and readied for consumption.

The Delicacies hung not only from the ceiling too, but even the walls were covered with Mr. Graves famous products that were served on a daily basis at His Meat Market and Deli.

There was So Much dripping Meat upon the walls; that the posters tacked to the structures supporting surface underneath the deli products, made it almost impossible to read the announcements that AWRS were trying to make.

There were even tubs of hamburger labeled for the shelters and someone's wedding.

Leaving the drugged, hurt and now unstrapped police officer to his own salvation, Jarrett proceeded into the room with all the meat. There was one other officer missing and since he wasn't out front, he must be in here.

And wouldn't you know it, the Detective's intuitions had been right once more.

Moving the racks out of his way after flipping on the light, JJ found what he was looking for.

He also discovered something that he was not expecting to find, the displayed skins of Mr. and Mrs. Graves. And that deduction was only provable because Skinner had Giant signs hanging over them labeled as Momma and Papa.

Jarrett also found Officer Rollins.

His dismembered body had been prepped for the grinder.

Portions of the ground man were already being seasoned for what appeared and smelled to be Salami.

That was also right about the time an Overpowering Smell of cinnamon engulfed JJ.

And with that smell, S.S.K. attacked the intruder who had So Rudely broke into his man cave.

As both men crashed upon the slaughter house floor of bloodied and human residual, the Detectives gun went sliding into an unknown corner of the meat filled room.

But that wasn't the only weapon in the room, JJ quickly found out.

The Butcher had knives laying on every counter.

As the two men slipped and slid back onto their feet, Mr. Graves was able to grab one of his favorite implements to work with.

A Massively Large carving knife.

The only thing JJ had been able to grasp in time was one of the meat racks that he was now having to use as a defensive shield.

Doing everything he could to keep the Serial Killer at bay; Officer Jefferson, "now fighting for his very life," was trying to force his way out of the room that had Only One Exit. Jarrett also needed to quickly grab for another rack of meat, after Skinner ripped that first one from his hands before Violently throwing it and its contents onto the floor.

That moment of surprise had also allowed JJ a few seconds to grasp a knife of his own as the floored meat now supplied an obstacle course of Watch Your Step.

While each man took turns slashing at the other, the approaching sirens were telling Mr. Graves that his moment to shine amongst Denver's Big Wigs and People To Be Seen With was coming to an end.

But, before Arapahoe's back-up team could arrive and aid JJ

in apprehending their suspect, Mr. Graves began to SCREAM while Intensively Clawing at the back of his head as he slid to the bloodied floor.

Jarrett was just about to consider the fact that his suspect was suffering from some sort of stroke, but what appeared in his unobstructed view quickly changed that opinion. There standing on his skinless feet with the mechanical lifts control box in his hand was Montezuma Counties drug induced Officer, Vance Thomas.

He had Violently Shoved the chains hooked end into the back of Skinner's skull.

And as the fact began to sink in that JJ's life had been saved by one of the men who had tried to set him up for murder, Skinner's ragged body started to stand up.

At first, that is what Arapahoe's startled Detective actually thought.

But once his feet left the ground, Mr. Jefferson realized that Vance was forcefully pressing the up button.

He did Almost have A Heart Attack Though when Skinner's dead body gave its last dying kicks of seizured viability. That Exact Moment he started walking away from The Monster who would later go down in the annuals of history as the one who turned an Entire City Into Cannibals.

That revelation was kept from the public by Arapahoe County for over Six Months.

Their reasoning as to why they didn't want to say just what Mr. Graves did with the missing bodies was unspeakable and begged the media and public to just drop it Please, but no one did.

Well, Eventually They Did Stop asking; but only after realizing not only what they had eaten themselves, but how does a person go about telling their Families, Friends and strangers that You fed them human flesh while they were partaking of Graves Meats at barbeques, gatherings and retreats.

The public soon learned that all homeless kitchens that had been receiving hamburger from the market, were now shut down too.

That count was estimated at just over One Hundred Shelters and close to Fifty Food Banks.

They no longer had a viable way of feeding the needy; and until someone else stepped up to the plate, they would never be opening again.

But back at Arapahoe's Investigative Department, the doors were open.

Except this time, the celebration concerning Skinners capture was an All Vegan affair.

No One was willing to take the chance ever again on a mom and Pop establishment.

S.S.K's capture also gave Detective Jarrett something he was not expecting; a department inquiry into his acting alone, under orders that Specifically Said Not Too.

That unwelcomed fiasco also came with a week off.

Something Jarrett's Best Friend was going To Make Sure that his buddy took full advantage of.

Two days later; just as Mr. Jefferson was about to settle in for the evening, there came a Very Hard knock on his front door.

Standing outside and looking all giddy and hyped up was John.

He also had something partially hidden in his left hand.

An Unredeemed Golden ticket to AWRS that had been upgraded to Platinum.

Against every wish and argument that JJ could come up with, Randal forced his friend to get dressed because he was taking Jarrett out to get laid. And if he refused to put some clothes on, Mr. Best Friend swore to his bud that he would have No Problem dragging his naked ass out of the house.

They were going and he just needed to kiss his opinion goodbye in this Boys Night Out matter.

Seeing that this was an unwinnable argument, the disgruntled Detective went ahead and got dressed, "making sure to take his concealed weapon," before climbing into Randal's car.

They were headed down into the Tech Area just off interstate Twenty-Five and East Belleview Avenue.

That's where AWRS had their Main room rental complex that came with your choice of an android companion. Something JJ would not be given as the two friends celebrated a night out on the town.

A Choice

Randal had JJ's sex bot all picked out after his Birthday Platinum Surprise Upgrade.

Something JJ wasn't Too Sure Of, after she walked into his private room.

The Synthetic was, "ALMOST," The Splitting Image of Jean.

The Detective actually considered leaving at that moment.

And he would have if she hadn't of reached over and touched him.

The robot's skin felt So Real against his.

Even her lips had that soft, moist feeling of kissing an actual person.

So Far, there wasn't anything about the fake human that felt toyish

If Jean's look alike hadn't of done what she did next, Mr. Jefferson would surely have left.

She began to run her hands inside his now unbuttoned shirt. Her soft touch was So Real.

And as his mind SCREAMED This Is Not Right, JJ took off her blouse and began to slowly stroke the units warm and subtle breast. The C-Cupped pair jiggled and bounced Just Like THE REAL THINGS as he began to squeeze and tweak the pair and their Hardening Nipples.

They also were, So, SO REAL.

As JJ pulled the unit into his arms, he was even More Amazed over the fact that her Entire Body was just as warm as his.

She even got goose bumps everywhere he touched her.

Something that was Totally Unexpected.

It wasn't until the synthetic noticed that her charge was

starting to tear up, that JJ Finally Realized just HOW REAL
They Were. The Android was concerned for his well-being
and was wondering if the Detective would be more
comfortable with the lights off.

An unexpected offer that JJ was More Than Willing to go
along with.

While the night progressed, Jarrett's anxiety over cheating
on his missing wife began to waiver.

There was just something so familiar about the way his robot
felt when he ran his hands over her skin, that the widower
finally decided it was time to let Jean Go. It has officially been
just over a year now and if she were going to return willingly, JJ
was Absolutely Certain that his Missing Wife would have done
it by now.

After accepting the fact that he was now All In, Mr. Jefferson
went for the gusto before sleepily cuddling next to the Real
Skinned robot.

And since checkout wasn't until Ten that following morning,
JJ had another round or two planned before he and Randal
walked out AWRS's whorehouse doors that offered any kind
of android one would want to choose for their sexual pleasure.

As the rays from the morning sun began to peak through a
partially opened curtain, JJ awoke to the backside of his warm
snuggle buddy. Since the synthetic was facing away and he
wasn't able to see her eyes, the Detective was wondering if she
were awake so that they could have sex again.

While he began to lightly run his hands along her right side;
the one sexually erotic body part that Jarrett craved the most
on a woman was her ass, and its delicacy just happened to be
out of reach.

That sweet buffet of pleasure was still hidden under the
covers.

And that's where the synthetic's butt should have stayed a
mystery.

Just as JJ's right hand began to remove the silk sheet, an
unexpected tattoo started to stare back at the Detective.

It's SHOCKING Revelation was a little more than he was

willing to handle at this point.

The Synthetic had THE EXACT SAME TATTOOED SAYING as JJ's missing wife.

This Ass belongs to Papi and No One Else.

As the startled Husband sat up in bed, his work phone began to ring.

It was Vickie Vawn from their crime lab. She was needing to speak with him, and its subject matter was URGENT.

Once Skinner's warehouse was processed, they found a set of light boxes containing the year Twenty Twenty-nine. And since that was the time Jean went missing, Vickie Declared that part of the evidence A Priority.

JJ, We Found Jeans skin sample labeled under the numbers Zero slash Seven slash Zero slash One slash Two slash Nine.

While Miss. Vawn proceeded to babble on about how sorry she was and to Please get with her if he needed to talk, the line at JJ's end went silent.

When he and Skinner were going at it, the man kept referring to just how much he loves the feel of Real Skin when it is being carved up. The one piece of evidence that they Never found amongst the Serial Killer's trophies.

The protective outer layer of his victims.

The department just assumed that it had been ground up in the meat, but all the body parts that were found had been skinned first.

So, just where did everyone's skin go.

The thought that occurred next was not one JJ was wanting to consider.

But being the Detective that he was, Jarrett just had to look for himself.

Years ago, "before Jean went missing," his wife had decided to take up Roller Blading. That fiasco had almost costed Mrs. Jefferson her Entire right ear.

Knowing the appendage had been reconnected by a Masterful plastic surgeon, only the Doc, Jean and JJ knew where the scar was hidden. So as not to be seen, he had magically sewn the imperfection into a hidden fold back behind the ear.

If someone didn't know where to exactly look, they would never find it.

But, Mr. Jefferson did know where to look.

And he was going to look right now.

Gently pulling the synthetic's ear away from the skulls right side, the now stretched out wrinkle revealed the Three-Inch-long scar that was hiding within.

It seemed that the answer to where the skins of Skinner's victims went, would be his final surprise.

And that discovery was just made by the Detective who caught him.

Once Vickie realized that she was talking to herself, the lab tech started listening in closely to what was taking place on the phone's other end. Detective Jarrett was mumbling to himself while it sounded as if he was also busily messing with something else.

The last thing Miss. Vawn testified about hearing before JJ's revolver went off, were these words.

Jean.

Jean.

Oh, Jean.

After that, the phone went dead.

As Vickie Vawn sat in the Chief's office reiterating her testimony to Commissioner Wess, Dutch, Judge Daily and the DA's Miss Garcia, AWRS's latest add began to play over the Office's public airwaves radio speaker.

At Androids With Real Skin, We now offer a Fantasy Line.

If You have a fever,

We Have The Doctor For You.

If Your Fiery Lust is out of hand,

This Fireman knows just how to quell those flames.

And if Your Desires are to be Handcuffed and Violated, Officer J with his handlebar Moustache is a Perfectionist at Cavity Searches.

Why Settle For

FAKE SKIN,

When You Can Have
REAL.
Look For A
REAL SKIN DEALER
Near You.